STORY OF O
Part II

'Both sexes are pulled in and turned on
when they look at this S&M classic.
Sometimes they become the exquisitely
submissive O, loving every abuse; several
pages later, they inexplicably become the
torturer' – *The Village Voice*

Return to the Château:
Story of O
Part II

preceded by
A Girl in Love

Pauline Réage

Translated from the
French by Sabine d'Estrée

CORGI BOOKS

STORY OF O PART II

A CORGI BOOK 0 552 12571 7

Originally published as *Retour à Roissy* by
Jean-Jacques Pauvert, éditeur, Paris, France.
Copyright © 1969 by Jean-Jacques Pauvert, éditeur.

First publication in Great Britain

PRINTING HISTORY
Corgi edition published 1985

Copyright © 1971 by Grove Press, Inc.

This book is set in 11/12 Century

Corgi Books are published by
Transworld Publishers Ltd.,
Century House, 61–63 Uxbridge Road,
Ealing, London W5 5SA

Made and printed in Great Britain by
Hunt Barnard Printing Ltd., Aylesbury, Bucks.

A Girl in LOVE

One day a girl in love said to the man she loved:

'I could also write the kind of stories you like . . .'

'Do you really think so?' he answered.

They met two or three times a week, but never during vacations, and never on weekends. Each of them stole the time they spent together from their families and their work. On afternoons in January and February, when the days begin to grow longer and the sun, sinking in the west, tints the Seine with red reflections, they used to walk along the banks of the river, the quai des Grands Augustins, the quai de la Tournelle, kissing in the shadow of the bridges. Once a *clochard* shouted at them:

'Shall we take up a collection and rent you a room?'

Their places of refuge often changed. The old car, which the girl drove, took them to the zoo to see the giraffes, to Bagatelle to see the irises and the clematis in the spring, or the asters in the fall. She noted the names of the asters—blue fog, purple, pale pink—and wondered why, since she was never able to plant them (and yet we shall have further occasion to refer to asters). But Vincennes, or the Bois de Boulogne, is a long way away. In the Bois you run into people who know you. Which, of course, left rented rooms. The same one several times in succession. Or different rooms, as chance would have it. There is a strange sweetness about the meager lighting of rented rooms in hotels near railroad stations: the modest luxury of the double bed, whose linen you leave unmade as you leave the room, has a charm all its own. And the time comes when you can no longer separate the sound of words and signs from the endless drone of the motors and the hiss of the tires climbing the street. For several years, these furtive and tender halts, in the respite that follows love, legs all entwined and arm unclasped, had been soothed by the kind of exchanges and as it were small talk in which books hold the most important place. Books were their only complete freedom, their common country, their true travels. Together they dwelt in the books they loved as others in their family home; in books they had their compatriots and their brothers; poets had written for them, the letters of lovers from times past came down to them through the obscurity of ancient languages, of modes and mores long since come and gone—all of which was read in a toneless voice in an unknown room, the sordid and miraculous dungeon against which the crowd outside, for a few short hours, beat in vain. They did not have a full night together. All of a sudden, at such and such an hour agreed upon ahead of time—the watch always remained on the wrist—they had to leave. Each had to regain his street, his house, his room, his daily bed, return to those to whom he was joined by another kind of inexpiable love, those whom fate, youth, or you yourself had given you once and for all, those whom you can neither leave nor hurt when you're involved in their lives. He, in his room, was not alone. She was alone in hers.

One evening, after that 'Do you really think

so?' of the first page, and without ever having the faintest idea that she would one day find the name Réage in a real estate register and would borrow a first name from two famous profligates, Pauline Borghese and Pauline Roland, one day this girl for whom I am speaking, and rightly so, since if I have nothing of hers she has everything of mine, the voice to begin with, one evening this girl, instead of taking a book to read before she fell asleep, lying on her left side with her feet tucked up under her, a soft black pencil in her right hand, began to write the story she had promised.

Spring was almost over. The Japanese cherry trees in the big Paris parks, the Judas trees, the magnolias near the fountains, the elder trees bordering the old embankments of the tram lines that used to encircle the city, had lost their flowers. The days lingered on forever, and the morning light penetrated at unwanted hours to the dusty black curtains of passive resistance, the last remaining vestiges of the war. But beneath the little lamp still lighted at the head of the bed, the hand holding the pencil raced over the paper without the least concern for the hour or the light. The girl was writing the way you speak in the dark to the person you love when you've held back the words of love too long and they flow at last. For the first time in her life she was writing without hesitation, without stopping, rewriting, or discarding, she was writing the way one breathes, the way one dreams. The constant hum of the cars grew fainter, one no longer heard the banging of doors, Paris was slipping into silence. She was still writing when the street cleaners came by, at the first touch of dawn. The first night entirely spent the way sleepwalkers doubtless spend theirs, wrested from herself or, who knows, returned to herself.

In the morning she gathered up the sheets of paper that contained the two beginnings with which you're already familiar, since if you are reading this it means you have already taken the trouble to read the entire tale and therefore know more about it today than she knew at that time. Now she had to get up, wash, dress, arrange her hair, resume the strict harness, the everyday smile, the customary silent sweetness. Tomorrow, no, the day after, she would give him the notebook.

She gave it to him as soon as he got into the car, where she was waiting for him a few yards from an intersection, on a small street near a *metro* station and an outdoor market. (Don't try and situate it, there are many like it, and what difference does it make anyway?) Read it immediately? Out of the question. Besides, this encounter turned out to be one of those where you come simply to say that you can't come, when you learn too late that you won't be able to make it and don't have time to tell the other party. It was already a stroke of luck that he had been able to get away at all. Otherwise she would have waited for an hour and then come back the following day at the same time, the same place, in accordance with the classic rules of clandestine lovers. He said 'get away' because they both used a vocabulary of prisoners whose prison does not revolt them, and perhaps they realized that if they found it hard to endure they would have found it just as hard to be freed from it, since they would then have felt guilty. The idea that they would have to return home gave a special meaning to that stolen time, which came to exist outside the pale of real time, in a sort of strange and eternal present. They should have felt hemmed in and hunted down as the years went winging by without bringing them any greater degree of freedom. But they did not. The daily, the weekly obstacles —frightful Sundays without any letters, or any phone calls, without any possible word or glance, frightful vacations a hundred thousand miles from anywhere, and always someone there to ask: 'A penny for your thoughts'—were more than enough to make them fret and worry and constantly wonder whether the other still felt the same way as before. They did not demand to be happy, but having once *known* each other, they simply asked with fear and trembling that it last, in the name of all that's holy that it last . . . that one not suddenly seem estranged from the other, that this unhoped-for fraternity, rarer than desire, more precious than love—or which perhaps at long last *was* love—should endure. So that everything was a risk: an encounter, a new dress, a trip, an unknown poem. But nothing could stand in the way of taking these risks. The most serious to date, nonetheless, was the notebook. And what if the phantasms that it revealed were to outrage her love or, worse, bore him or, worse yet, strike him as being ridiculous? Not for that they were, of course, but because they emanated from her, and because one rarely forgives in those one loves the vagaries or excesses one readily forgives in others. She was wrong to be afraid: 'Ah, keep at it,' he said. What happens after that? Do you know? She knew. She discovered it by slow degrees. During the rest of the waning summer, throughout the fall, from the torrid beaches of some dismal watering spot until her return to a russet and burnt-out Paris, she wrote what she knew. Ten pages at a time, or five, full chapters or fragments of chapters, she

13

slipped her pages, the same size as the original
notebook, written sometimes in pencil, sometimes in ink, whether ballpoint or the fine point of
a real fountain pen, into envelopes and addressed
them to the same General Delivery address. No
carbon copy, no first draft: she kept nothing.
But the postal service came through. The story
was still not completely written when, having
resumed their assignations back in Paris in the
fall, the man asked her to read sections out loud
to him, as she wrote them. And in the dark car, in
the middle of an afternoon on some bleak but
busy street, near the Buttes-aux-Cailles, where
you have the feeling you're transported back to
the last years of the previous century, or on the
banks of the St. Martin Canal, the girl who was
reading had to stop, break off, once or more than
once, because it is possible silently to imagine the
worst, the most burning detail, but not read out
loud what was dreamt in the course of intermin-
able nights.

And yet one day the story did stop. Before O,
there was nothing further that that death toward
which she was vaguely racing with all her might
could do, that death which is granted her in two
lines. As for revealing how the manuscript came
into the hands of Jean Paulhan, I promised not to
reveal it, as I promised not to divulge the real
name of Pauline Réage, counting on the courtesy
and integrity of those who are privy to it to keep
the secret as long as I feel bound not to break that
promise. Besides, nothing is more fallacious and
shifting than an identity. If you believe, as hun-
dreds of millions of men do, that we live several
lives, why not also believe that in each of our lives
we are the meeting place for several souls? 'Who
am I, finally,' said Pauline Réage, 'if not the long

silent part of someone, the secret and nocturnal part which has never betrayed itself in public by any thought, word, or deed, but communicates through the subterranean depths of the imaginary with dreams as old as the world itself?' Whence came to me those oft-repeated reveries, those slow musings just before falling asleep, always the same ones, in which the purest and wildest love always sanctioned, or rather always demanded, the most frightful surrender, in which childish images of chains and whips added to constraint the symbols of constraint, I'm not sure which. All I know is that they were beneficent and protected me mysteriously—contrary to all the reasonable reveries that revolve around our daily lives, trying to organize it, to tame it. I have never known how to tame my life. And yet it seemed indeed as though these strange dreams were a help in that direction, as though some ransom had been paid by the delirium and delights of the impossible: the days that followed were oddly lightened by them, whereas the orderly arrangement of the future and the best—laid plans founded on good common sense proved each time to be contradicted by the event itself. Thus I learned at a very tender age that you should not spend the empty hours of the night building dream castles, nonexistent but possible, workable, where friends and relatives would be happy together (how fanciful!)—but that one could without fear build and furnish clandestine castles, on the condition that you people them with girls in love, prostituted by love, and triumphant in their chains. So it was that Sade's castles, discovered long after I had silently built my own, never surprised me, as I was not surprised by the discovery of his society, The Friends of Crime: I already had my own secret society, however minor and inoffensive. But Sade made me understand that we are all jailers, and all in prison, in that there is always someone within us whom we enchain, whom we imprison, whom we silence. By a curious kind of reverse shock, it can happen that prison itself can open the gates to freedom. The stone walls of a cell, the solitude, but also the night, the solitude, again the solitude, the warmth of the sheets, the silence, free this unknown creature whom we have kept locked up. It escapes us and escapes endlessly, through the walls, the ages, the interdictions. It passes from one to the other, from one age to another, from one country to another, it assumes one name or another. Those who speak in its behalf are merely translators who, without knowing why (why them, why that particular moment in time?), have been allowed, for one brief moment, to seize a few strands of this immemorial network of forbidden dreams. So that, fifteen years ago, why not me?

'What intrigued and excited him, I mean the person for whom I was writing this story,' she went on, 'was the relationship it might have with my own life. Could it be that the story was the deformed, the inverted image of my life? That it was the shadow of it borne, unrecognizable, confined like that of some stroller in the midday sun, or otherwise unrecognizable, diabolically elongated like the shadow that stretches before someone walking back from the Altantic Ocean, over the empty beach, as the setting sun goes down in flames behind him? I saw, between what I thought myself to be and what I was relating and thought I was making up, both a distance so radical and a kinship so profound that I was incapable of recognizing myself in it. I no doubt accepted my life with such patience (or passivity, or weakness) only because I was so certain of being able to find whenever I wanted that other, obscure life that is life's consolation, that other life unacknowledged and unshared—and then all of a sudden thanks to the man I loved I did acknowledge it, and hence-forth would share it with any and all, as perfectly prostituted in the anonymity of a book as, in the book, that faceless, ageless, nameless (even first-nameless) girl. Never did he ask any questions about her. He knew that she was an idea, a figment, a sorrow, the negation of a destiny. But the others? René Jacqueline, Sir Stephen, Anne-Marie? And what about the places, the streets, the gardens, the houses, Paris, Roissy? And what about the circum-stances, the events themselves? For these, yes, I thought I knew. René, for example (a nostalgic first name), was the remembrance, no, the vestige of an adolescent love, rather the hope of a love that never happened, and René had never had the slightest suspicion that I might be capable of loving him. But Jacqueline had loved him. And before she loved him, she had loved me. She had in fact been responsible for being the first to break my heart. Fifteen, we were both fifteen, and she had spent the entire school year chasing me, complaining about my coldness. No sooner had summer vacation come and whisked her away than I awakened from this lack of interest, this coldness. I wrote her. July, August, Sep-tember: for three full months I watched and waited for the postman, but in vain. And still I wrote. Those letters proved my undoing. Jacqueline's parents stopped her from seeing me, and it was from her, enrolled in another division, that I learned that 'that was a sin.' That what was a sin? What did they have against me? The day is not more chaste ... I had reinvented Rosalinde and Celia, in all innocence—who did not last. The

17

fact remains that Jacqueline, this real Jacqueline, figures in the story only by her first name and her fair hair. The one in the story is rather a young actress, pale and overbearing, with whom I lunched one day somewhere on the rue de l'Éperon. The old man who gave her her jewels, her dresses, her car, took me aside and said: 'She's beautiful, isn't she?' Yes, she was beautiful. I never saw her again. Is René what I might have become had I been a man? Devoted to another, to the point of yielding everything to him, without even finding it anachronistic, this vassal-to-lord relationship? I'm afraid the answer is yes. Whereas the imaginary Jacqueline was the stranger par excellence. It took me a long time to realize, however, that in another life a girl like her—one whom I admired unequivocally— had taken my lover away from me. And I took my revenge by shipping her off to Roissy, I who pretended to disdain any form of vengeance, I took revenge and wasn't even capable of realizing it. To make up a story is a curious trap. As for Sir Stephen, I saw him, literally, in the flesh. My current lover, the one I just mentioned, pointed him out to me one afternoon in a bar near the Champs Elysées: half—seated on a stool at the mahogany bar, silent, self-composed, with that air of some gray-eyed prince that fascinates both men and women—he pointed him out to me and said: 'I don't understand why women don't prefer men like him to boys under thirty.' At the time he was under thirty. I didn't respond. But they do prefer them. I stared for a long time at the unknown man, who wasn't even looking at me. Fifty years old probably, an Englishman certainly. And what else? Nothing. But this silent, unilateral rapport between him and my companion, between him and me, reappeared out of the blue ten years later, in the middle of the night pierced by the light of my table lamp, and the hand on the paper brought him back to life with a new meaning even quicker than reflection. Anne-Marie, I don't know at all. One of my woman friends (whom I respect, and I am slow to respect) might well be Anne-Marie were it not for the fact that she is the epitome of purity and honor: I mean that Anne-Marie might have got from her her rigor and her resolve, her free and easy manner, and straightforward, unequivocal way in which she exercised her profession. To tell the truth, the professions in question (O's and Anne-Marie's, prostitute or procuress, to make things utterly clear) are outside my sphere of knowledge. A major writer outraged by the publication of O thought he saw in my story the memoirs of a courtesan—admitting by way of excuse that he had not read the book—but he was wrong on two scores: they are not memoirs, and I am not a courtesan, however delicate the expression may be. Let us say so as not to offend him that it was doubtless a matter of having missed my chosen calling. After the abbreviated cast of characters, as at the theater, is there any point in clarifying the places where the action occurs? They belong to everyone. The rue de Poitiers and the private room at La Perouse, the room in the whore-house-hotel near the Bastille, with its mirror on the ceiling, the streets in the vicinity of St. Germain, the sun-drenched quays of the île St. Louis, the dry, whitened stones of the back country of Provence, and this Roissy-en-France glimpsed during a brief excursion one spring, scarcely more than a place-name on a map—of course nothing is made up, not anymore than the asters which I said earlier we would have occasion to mention again. Nor did I make up—steal, rather, for which I ask her belated pardon, but the theft was committed out of admiration—the Leonor Fini masks. I also, it would seem, stole a lady's living room, for some unspeakable purpose: Sir Stephen's living room, no less! She told me so herself, not realizing of course to whom she was speaking (one never knows to *whom* one is speaking). Never have I set foot in that lady's house, never have I laid eyes on her living room. Nor had I ever seen (and did not even know it existed) the house hidden in a hollow where for years a girl whom I subsequently chanced to meet gave exhibitions for the man she loved—who watched her with the help of a one-way mirror and a microphone hidden in the wall— the same kind of exhibitions that Sir Stephen demanded from O: surrender to complete strangers, recruited by him, imposed by him. No, I did not copy her story: no, she did not model her own actions after the one I wrote. But once having taken into account the fair share played by the fantastic and fanciful, and by the endless repetition, in the assuagement of obsessions (the endless repetition of pleasures and brutality being as necessary as it is absurd and impossible to achieve) everything blends together faithfully, dreamed or experienced, everything unfolds as being commonly shared in the universe of a like madness—and if you manage to look at them squarely—horrors, wonders, dreams, and lies— everything there is conjuration and release.

PAULINE RÉAGE

20

Return to the Château

The pages that follow are a sequel to *Story of O*. They deliberately suggest the degradation of that work, and cannot under any circumstances be integrated into it.

P.R.

I

Thus, everything seemed to be settled: September was just around the corner. In the middle of September O was to return to Roissy, taking Natalie with her, while René, after his return from a trip to North Africa, would take Jacqueline —at least he intimated as much. How long Natalie would be kept there, and how long O, would doubtless depend, for O, on whatever decision Sir Stephen might make, and, for Natalie, on what masters, or master, fate would hold in store for her at Roissy. But in this calm of well-laid plans O felt uneasy, as though she had some foreboding of danger, as though fate was being tempted, about this selfsame certainty that everyone around her felt that things would come to pass just as they had planned. Natalie's happiness was equalled only by her impatience, and there was, in that happiness, a fair measure of the naïveté and confidence that children display when they have been promised something by adults. It was not the sway that Sir Stephen held over her, and that O freely acknowledged, that might have awakened the slightest suspicion of doubt in Natalie: O's submission was so absolute and so constantly immediate that Natalie was quite incapable of conceiving, so great was her admiration for O, that anyone might ever contradict or disagree with Sir Stephen, since O knelt down before him. No matter how happy O may have been, and precisely because she was happy, she was reluctant to believe it, nor did she dare to temper Natalie's impatience, or to dampen her joy. From time to time, though, when Natalie would begin humming or singing softly to herself, O would make her stop, in order to ward off fate. She was careful never to step on the cracks in the floor, never to spill any salt, cross knives, or walk under ladders. And what Natalie did not know, and O did not dare to tell her, was that, if she took such great pleasure in being whipped, it was—aside from the physical enjoyment she derived from it to some degree—because of the happiness she experienced at being surrendered to a will above and beyond her own—beyond this point she paid for it as it were in pain and humiliation—humiliation because she could not cry out and beg for mercy even as she was experiencing pleasure, thereby perhaps superstitiously guaranteeing that the flogging would not be cut short. Ah, to remain motionless so that time stops too! O loathed dawn and dusk, when everything shifts, when everything exchanges one shape for another, so sadly, so perfidiously. Didn't the fact that René had given her to Sir Stephen, as well as her own ease at shifting from one to the other, make it just as likely that Sir Stephen might also change? Standing naked one day in front of her chest of drawers, whose bronze statues were fake Chinese, with their pointed hats like the beach hats Natalie wore, O suddenly realized that there was something new about Sir Stephen's attitude toward her. First of all, he required her to be constantly naked in her room. Even her bedroom slippers were henceforth forbidden, as were any necklaces and jewelry. It was nothing. If Sir Stephen, far from the château at

Roissy, felt like instituting a rule that reminded him of Roissy, why should O be surprised? But there were other, more serious signs. To be sure, O fully expected, the night of the ball, that Sir Stephen would turn her over to his host. To be sure, he himself—in René's presence, for instance, or in Anne-Marie's, and certainly, more recently, in Natalie's—had already possessed her in full daylight. But prior to that night he had never allowed himself to be present while she was being possessed by someone else, nor had he shared her with the person to whom he had offered her. Nor had Sir Stephen ever offered her to someone else without having punished her afterward, as though his very purpose in prostituting her had been to find a pretense to punish her. But the day after the ball he had not. Was it that the shame O felt in being taken by someone else in Sir Stephen's presence might have appeared to him to represent sufficient redemption in itself? What she had so unflinchingly accepted when it had happened with René rather than with Sir Stephen, what she accepted unquestioningly when Sir Stephen was not there, had seemed to O loathsome with him present.

After that, two days went by without Sir Stephen seeing her. O wanted to send Natalie back to her room; Sir Stephen forbade her from doing so. Thus O waited until Natalie was asleep before she broke down and wept bitter tears, silently, without anyone awake to see her. It was only on the fourth day that Sir Stephen came into her room, as was his wont, as the afternoon was drawing to a close, took her and allowed himself to be caressed by her. When at last he moaned and in his pleasure cried out her name, she saw herself saved. But when she whispered to him, stretched out full—length beside him, golden and dead on the white rug, when she asked him in a near whisper whether he loved her he did not say: 'I love you, O,' but only: 'Of course,' and laughed. But did he really?

'You will be at Roissy on September 15,' he had said.

'Without you?' O had said.

'Oh, I'll be along in due time,' he had answered.

It was then near the end of August: the figs, the dark grapes in baskets, attracted wasps; the sun was less bright, and threw longer shadows at nightfall. O was alone in the big, dry house, with Natalie and Sir Stephen. René had gone away with Jacqueline.

Did O have to take to counting the days that separated her from September 15, as Natalie did—fourteen more, twelve more—or was that due date one to be feared? These days, so carefully counted, slipped by in silence. Natalie and O were locked as though it had been planned beforehand in a Gynaeceum from which they had no desire to be freed, where the only sound, so completely did the walls muffle the words and laugher, was O screaming whenever she was beaten. One Sunday evening, when the sky was overcast and a storm brewing, Sir Stephen sent word to O to dress and come downstairs. She had heard a car door slamming, and through the bathroom window, which looked out onto the courtyard, the sounds of voices. Then nothing more. Natalie had come racing upstairs to tell her that she had caught a glimpse of the visitors: there were three of them in all, one of whom must have been Malaysian, to judge by his complexion and pitch-black eyes: he was tall, thin, and handsome. They were not speaking French, or English; Natalie thought it must have been German. German or not, O did not understand a word they were saying. And what was she to make of Sir Stephen's indifference? It wasn't that he pretended not to look at her; on the contrary, he laughed and no doubt exchanged witty remarks with his guests while they were using her, but so completely at ease and with such an obvious air of detachment that O felt she might well have preferred contempt, or at least a feeling of resentment on his part, to this sudden absence, as though even while he was with her she no longer existed for him. It was contempt, and a curious pity that she found even more intolerable, that O read in the eyes of the Malaysian, who had not touched her, as she freed herself from the hands of the other two men, dishevelled and out of breath, her skirt full of spots. They must have found her to their taste, since they came back alone the next day about eleven o'clock. This time Sir Stephen dispensed with ceremony and had them go right up to her room, where she was naked.

After they left, O broke down and began to sob. 'Why, O?' Sir Stephen wanted to know. But he knew very well why; and how could O blot out of her memory the feeling of despair she felt when she saw herself, in her own room, and in his presence, being treated in a way few whores were treated in the meanest brothels, and, worst of all, being treated by him as though he took her for one. He told her that she could not be the judge of where, how, and for whom she was to serve, as she could not be the judge of his feelings. Then he had her whipped, so cruelly that for a fleeting moment she was comforted by it. But there was no getting around the fact that, once her tears were dry and the searing pain had subsided, she found herself prey once again to the feeling that had terrified her: that some other reason than the pleasure he might derive from it—and did he indeed still derive any? made him prostitute her, and that she was useful to him as some kind of not-so-legal tender: but to be tendered in exchange for what? A terrible, grotesque image crossed her mind: the calvary of Saint George. Yes, perhaps she was the lowest representation of that same calvary, on her knees and supported by her elbows, straddled by unknown men. And if he had her beaten, it was no longer for any other reason than to improve her training. If that were true, then why was she complaining, why was she so surprised and upset? Still tied to the balustrade next to her bed where it would seem that Sir Stephen had decided to leave her, and where indeed he did leave her for nearly three hours, O heard his voice echoing in her memory, that same voice that had made such a lasting and profound effect upon her on that first evening when he had taken her, had slapped her, had lacerated her loins, when he had told her that he wanted to obtain, and would obtain, from her, by submission and pure obedience, what she thought she would grant only through love. Whose fault was it, other than her own, if all it took him was a whipping to make her automatically give herself to him? If she had to hold someone in abhorrence, wasn't it wrong to blame anyone but herself? And if he was using her for some purpose other than his pleasure, what business was it of hers? 'Ah, yes,' O said to herself, 'I find myself disgusting. How can I have the gall to complain about being betrayed; haven't I been warned a hundred times, a thousand; do I still not know why I was born?' But she was no longer certain, it was no longer clear in her own mind, whether she was disgusted with herself for being a slave—or because she wasn't slavish enough. But it was neither one nor the other. She held herself in abhorrence because she was no longer loved. What had she done, what had she failed to do, to deserve such a shift in Sir Stephen's affections? You're out of your mind, O, as though it had something to do with you, as though you had any say in the matter. The irons that lay heavy on her belly, the brand which had been seared into the flesh of her buttocks, were for her, had always been for her, marks of pride, because they proclaimed that the person who had imposed them upon her loved her enough to set her thus apart from all others. Would she now feel obliged to be ashamed of them or, if he no longer loved her, would they still remain as the proof that she still belonged to him? For it was apparent that he still wanted her to belong to him.

II

September 15 arrived; O, Natalie, and Sir Stephen were still there. But now it was Natalie's turn to be in tears: her mother had sent for her, and she would have to go back to her boarding school at the end of the month. If O was to go to Roissy, she would go alone. Sir Stephen found O seated in her armchair, with the child on the floor beside her, her head buried in O's lap, sobbing. O handed him the letter Natalie had received: Natalie would have to be leaving in two days.

'But you promised, you promised,' the child kept saying over and over.

'It's just not possible, little one,' Sir Stephen said.

'You could make it possible if you really wanted to,' Natalie insisted.

Sir Stephen made no response. O was gently stroking the silken hair that bathed her bare knees. The fact of the matter was, if Sir Stephen had really wanted to, O could probably have found some way to persuade Natalie's mother to let her keep the child with her for another two weeks or so, under the pretense of taking her to the country outside Paris. It would not have taken much: one letter, or at most a visit from O. And in two weeks, Natalie . . .

What it meant was that Sir Stephen had changed his mind. He was standing by the window, gazing out at the garden. O bent down over the child, lifted her head, and kissed both her tear-filled eyes. She glanced quickly: Sir Stephen had not moved an inch. She took Natalie's mouth. It was Natalie's moan that caught Sir Stephen's attention and made him turn back to them. But O remained seemingly oblivious and slipped down beside her, so that they were both lying side by side on the rug. Two steps, and Sir Stephen was standing over them. O heard him striking a match and smelled the acrid odor of his cigarette. He smoked dark-tobaccoed Gaulloise blue, like a Frenchman. Natalie's eyes were closed.

'Undress her, O, and caress her,' he said suddenly. 'Then you can turn her over to me. But first open her up a little. I don't want to hurt her too much.'

Was that it? Oh, if all he wanted was Natalie, if that was all she had to give him! Was he in love with her? It seemed rather that he wanted, just as she was about to disappear, to bring something to an end, to destroy a fantasy. Well-rounded and soft, Natalie was nonetheless slender, and slightly shorter than O. Sir Stephen seemed twice her size. Without moving a muscle, she allowed herself to be undressed by O, allowed herself to be brought to the bed, which O had opened and turned down; without moving a muscle she allowed herself to be caressed, moaning faintly when O touched her or stroked her gently, gritting her teeth when O was more brutal. It was not long before O's hand was covered with blood. But Natalie refrained from crying out until the full weight of Sir Stephen was upon her. It was the first time that O saw Sir Stephen deriving pleasure from someone other than herself, and more simply because she could see the expression on his face in the throes of pleasure. How he fled!

Yes, he held Natalie's head against his loins, his hands grasping fistfuls of hair, as he did with O's hair; O persuaded herself that it was only to feel more fully and intimately the mouth that encompassed him, until he found release within it, but any mouth, provided it was docile and ardent enough, would have provided him with similar satisfaction, with like release. Natalie did not count. Was O all that sure that she counted?

'I love you,' she whispered over and over again, too softly for him to hear it. 'I love you,' using the formal 'vous' rather than the familiar 'tu.' Even in her thoughts and whispers she didn't dare use the familiar form with him. Sir Stephen's head was thrown back, and his gray eyes were nearly closed, like two slits of light. Between his slightly parted lips, his teeth also gleamed. For a moment he seemed disarmed, defenseless, but as soon as he felt O looking at him he caught himself, left the current into which he was slipping, a current into which O thought she had so often in the past slipped with him, stretched out beside him on that bark where lovers drift. But it was probably not true. They had probably been alone, each in his own way, and perhaps there was nothing fortuitous about the fact that each time he sank within her his face was averted from her; perhaps he wanted to be alone, and today was the accident, the rule rather than the exception. O saw this as a fatal sign: the sign that his feelings for her had withered to such a state of indifference that he no longer even took the trouble to turn his head. It was impossible, in any case, no matter how one interpreted it, not to see in his act an assurance, a freedom which ought to have, were it not for the very doubts she felt as to whether she was loved at all, made her giddy, proud, content, happy. She told herself as much.

When Sir Stephen left her, with Natalie curled up in her arms still burning and murmuring with pride, O watched her fall asleep, then gently drew the sheets and a light blanket up over her. No, he wasn't in love with Natalie. But he was absent, as absent from himself, perhaps, as he was from her. Somewhere else.

O had never really given any thought to deducing what Sir Stephen's profession was, or even whether he had one, and René had never talked about it. It was obvious that he was wealthy, in that mysterious way English aristocrats are wealthy, when they still are. Where did his money come from? René worked for an export-import company; René used to say, 'I have to make a business trip to Algiers to see about some jute'; 'I have to fly over to London about some woollen goods, or china'; 'I have to run down to Spain to buy some copper.' René had an office, business associates, employees. She may not have been very clear as to the exact nature of his job, or the title he held, but the job did exist and the obligations it entailed were strikingly apparent. Perhaps Sir Stephen had some position too, one that might explain his trips, his prolonged stays in Paris and, thought O, not without a feeling of dread, his connection with Roissy (a connection which in René's case struck her as being no more or less than the result of a chance encounter—'I happened to run into a friend one day and he took me there,' he used to tell her—and O believed him). What did she know about Sir Stephen? That he belonged to the Campbell clan and was thus a descendant of the earls of Argyll. That their somber plaid, with its black, blue-black, and green colors, was the most beautiful of all Scotland, and the most infamous (the Campbells betrayed the Stuarts, and the ninth earl of Argyll

38

was captured and beheaded, in 1685). That he owned a castle somewhere in the northwest corner of Scotland overlooking the Irish Sea, a small, compact granite castle built in the French manner by some eighteenth-century ancestor and looking for all the world like some St. Malo château. But what native of St. Malo had ever had, as a setting for his château, vast greenswards steeped in the morning dew, or as a sheath for its walls lush layers of Scottish ivy?

'I'll take you there next year, with Anne-Marie,' Sir Stephen had said one day as he was showing her photos of the place.

Who lived in the castle? What kind of family did he have, if indeed he had one? O suspected that he had been, and perhaps still was, a professional career officer. A number of his compatriots who were younger than he invariably addressed him as 'Sir,' nothing more, the way a subordinate speaks to a superior. O was well aware that there still exists in the British Isles a prejudice, or a peculiar custom, whereby a man is bound not to talk about either his wife or his business, about his profession or about money. Out of respect? Out of contempt? It was impossible to say. But it was also impossible to complain about it. And so O did not. She would simply have liked to feel certain that Sir Stephen's silence concerning her was part and parcel of this same British quality or custom. And at the same time she secretly wanted him to break his silence, so that she could reassure him that if he had the slightest problem, the slightest worry, she was ready and willing to help him, if it was within her power to do so, in any way.

III

The day following the departure of Natalie—for whom they had booked a sleeper on the *Train Bleu*—and two days before the departure of O and Sir Stephen, who were taking the train together back to Paris—but Sir Stephen had specified that it be such and such a date, and not the same day as Natalie's departure, as he had specified in no uncertain terms that they return by train, and by that particular train, rather than by car—O finally managed to say to him, while they were finishing breakfast, which they had taken alone together, and as old Norah was bringing in the coffee, O, emboldened because when she had got up and passed close to where he was sitting he had, mechanically perhaps, the way one does to a dog or cat, caressed her buttocks, O finally managed to say to him, in a voice so low it was scarcely audible, that she was afraid she was a source of irritation, of displeasure, to him, but that she wanted to assure him that she would serve him in any way he wanted. He looked at her tenderly at first, then had her kneel down while he kissed her breasts; then, after she had got back up and was standing beside him, his expression changed.

'I know,' he said. 'The two men the other day . . .'

'The Germans?' O broke in.

'They aren't German,' said Sir Stephen, 'but that's not the point. I just wanted to warn you that one of them will be travelling in the same train with us. We'll have dinner together in the dining car. Please make a special effort to be pretty so that he'll desire you, and follow you back to your compartment.'

'But he knows very well,' O said, 'that you're the one who determines what I do or don't do.'

'Of course he does,' Sir Stephen went on. 'We have adjoining compartments. He'll come in through mine to yours.'

'Whatever you say,' O said, and did not ask what the reason was—certain as she was that this time there was a reason—despondent at being unable to rid herself of the notion that, if Sir Stephen had prostituted her the other times for no reason, and as it were gratuitously, it was less in order to accustom her to the idea than to sow confusion and make her the instrument, the blind instrument, of something other than his own pleasure.

IV

The *Train Bleu* was due to arrive in Paris about nine o'clock in the morning. At about eight, O, prey to a kind of indifference which she completely failed to understand but which created an armored seal around her heart, had walked steadily on her high heels down the corridors that separated her compartment from the dining car, where she had drunk the too-bitter coffee and eaten the eggs and bacon which constituted the breakfast fare. Sir Stephen had sat down across from her. The eggs were stale and tasteless: the smell of cigarettes, the swaying movement of the train, all contributed to make O slightly nauseous. But when the pseudo-German arrived to join them and sat down next to Sir Stephen, neither his open stare that fixed itself on O's lips, nor the memory of the meekness with which she had caressed him during the previous night, disturbed her. Something, she didn't quite know what, protected her, left her free to watch the woods and fields slip by beside her, to look for the names of the wayside stations. The trees and the fog concealed the houses set back any distance from the tracks; tall iron pylons, set in concrete bases, flashed by periodically, incongruous in the pastoral setting; one could scarcely make out the electric wires that passed from one to the other, every three hundred yards as far as the

47

eye could see. At Ville-neuve-Saint-Georges Sir
Stephen suggested to O that they return to their
compartments. His neighbor, scrambling to his
feet, clicked his heels and almost split himself in
two bidding O good-bye. A sudden jolt of the train
made him lose his balance and sent him sprawling
back into his seat. O could not keep from laughing. Was she surprised when Sir Stephen—who
had completely ignored her since the start of the
journey—had her bend down over the suitcases
piled pell-mell on the compartment seat, virtually
the minute they were back inside, and raised her
pleated skirt? She was delighted, and grateful.
To anyone who might have seen her in this position, kneeling on the compartment seat, her
breasts crushed against the baggage, completely
dressed, but offering, between the hem of her
suitcoat and her stockings, and the black garter
belt to which they were fastened, her bare
buttocks crisscrossed with leatherlike stripes, to
anyone who might have seen her thus she could
only have seemed ridiculous, and she was well
aware of it. She could never help remembering,
whenever she was thus made to lie prone, the disturbing, but also the humiliating and ridiculous
aspect of the expression 'lift your skirt,' even
more humiliating than that other expression
which Sir Stephen, as René before him, employed
at least each time he offered her to someone. This
feeling of humiliation that Sir Stephen, or rather
Sir Stephen's words, caused her each time he
uttered them, was soothing to her. But this
sweetness was as nothing compared to the happiness, mixed with pride, one might almost say
with glory, that overwhelmed her whenever he
deigned to seize and possess her, whenever he
found her body to his liking sufficiently to enter it
and, for a fleeting moment, dwell therein; it

seemed to O that no submission, no humiliation, would ever compensate him fairly for these precious moments.

All the time he held her transfixed, poised against him and jostled gently by the movement of the train, she moaned. It was only when the cars collided noisily against each other, as the train ground to a halt at the Gare de Lyon, that he slipped from her and told her to straighten up.

V

As they emerged from the station onto the cobblestone courtyard, from which the stairways descend to street level and which serves as a parking lot, a young man dressed in the uniform of a noncommissioned Air Force officer stepped forward from where he was standing near a black Citroën, which was locked, as soon as he saw Sir Stephen. He saluted, opened the door, and stood aside. When O was settled in the back seat, with the baggage in the front seat, Sir Stephen bent down just long enough to kiss her hand and smile, before closing the door. He had said nothing to her, neither 'Good-bye,' nor 'I'll see you in a few days,' nor even 'Good-bye forever.' O had thought that he was going to join her in the back seat. The car started off so suddenly and at such speed that she did not have the presence of mind to call out to him, and although she threw herself against the back window in an effort to make some kind of sign to him, it was too late: his back was already turned to her and he was giving some instructions to his porter. Suddenly, like someone removing a bandage from a wound, the indifference which had protected her throughout the trip was stripped away and a single phrase began to dance through her head, over and over and over again: 'He didn't say good-bye to me.

He didn't even look at me.'

The Citroën moved swiftly westward leaving Paris behind; O was oblivious to the world outside the car. She was crying. Her face was still covered with tears when, half an hour later, the car turned off the main route and entered a forest road, over which tall beech trees cast dark shadows. It was raining, and the insides of the car windows, all of which were rolled up tightly, were steamed up. The driver tilted the back of the front seat until it was horizontal, then made O lie down upon it. The car had so little head room that O's feet touched the ceiling when he raised her legs to penetrate her. He spent almost an hour using her at will, and the thought did not even cross her mind to try and escape his embrace, so convinced was she that he had a perfect right to do what he was doing, and the only comfort she derived from the state of anxiety into which Sir Stephen's sudden departure had plunged her was the total silence which accompanied the young man's endeavors as he took her again and again, a silence broken only by a brief spasmodic moan at the moment of pleasure, until he had exhausted his forces.

He was perhaps twenty-five, with a thin, harsh yet sensitive face, in which two black eyes were set like somber jewels. He had, on two occasions, wiped O's tear-stained cheek with one finger, but at no time had he brought his mouth close to hers. It was obvious that he did not dare, although he did not have the slightest compunction about thrusting a sex so thick and so long in its state of erection that each time he rammed it home a fresh cascade of tears poured down her cheeks. When at last he had finished, O pulled down her skirt, rebuttoned first her sweater then her suit jacket, which she had opened so that he could have free access to her breasts: she had time, while he disappeared somewhere into the underbrush, to run a comb through her dishevelled hair, powder her face, and freshen the lipstick on her lips. The rain had stopped, the trunks of the beech trees shone brightly in the gray light. Almost touching the left side of the car, crowning a gentle slope, a red mass of foxgloves lay within arm's reach, so close that O could literally have reached out and picked them through the lowered window of the car. The driver returned, got into the car and closed the door which he had left open when he had disappeared, and started the motor. Once they had rejoined the main highway it was no more than fifteen minutes before they reached a little village that O did not recognize; but when the Citroën slowed down, after having skirted the length of some endless wall enclosing a vast park, and stopped before an ivy-covered house, O finally realized that it must indeed be the back entrance to Roissy. She got out of the car; the driver began busying himself with her baggage. The heavy wooden door, which was painted a dark green then varnished, opened even before she had a chance to knock or ring: they had seen her from inside. She crossed the threshold; the tiled vestibule, with its red and white muslin drapes, was empty. Directly opposite her, a mirror that covered the entire wall reflected her full-length portrait, thin and erect in her gray suit, her top coat over her arm, her suitcases piled around her feet, the door closing behind her, and this sprig of heather she was holding in her hand, a sprig she had automatically accepted when the driver had handed it to her, a childish and ridiculous keep-sake, which she did not dare throw onto the brightly waxed tile floor and which, for some reason she did not understand, embarrassed her. But yes, she did know. Who was it who had told her that heather picked in the woods near Paris brought bad luck? She would have been better off to have picked the foxgloves that her grandmother had forbidden her to touch as a child, because they are poisonous. She put the sprig of heather down on the windowsill of the only window in the vestibule. Just as she did, Anne-Marie, followed by a man dressed in a gardener's blue denim work clothes, came in. The gardener took O's suitcases.

'Don't tell me you finally made it,' said Anne-Marie. 'Sir Stephen called me almost two hours ago saying you were on your way. The car was supposed to bring you here directly. What happened?'

'It was the driver,' said O, 'I thought that . . .'

Anne-Marie burst out laughing. 'I get the picture,' she said. 'He raped you, and you let him do whatever he liked? No, that was not in the plans; he had no right to do what he did. But it doesn't matter, that's what you're here for.' And she added: 'You're off to a good start. I'm going to tell Sir Stephen what happened. It will give him a good laugh.'

'Is he going to come?' O inquired.

'I think so,' Anne-Marie said, 'but he didn't say when.'

The lump in O's throat when she had asked the question slowly dissolved, and she glanced at Anne-Marie gratefully; how lovely she was, how sparkling with her hair streaked with gray. She was wearing, over her black pants and matching blouse, a bright red jacket. Obviously, the rules which governed the dress and conduct of the women at Roissy did not apply to her.

'Today I want you to have lunch with me,' she said to O. 'Meanwhile, get yourself ready. On the stroke of three o'clock I'll take you to the little gate.'

O followed Anne-Marie without uttering a word; she was floating on cloud nine: Sir Stephen had said he would come.

VI

Anne-Marie's apartment occupied part of a separate wing, a prolongation of the château proper constructed in the direction of the main highway. It consisted of a living room which communicated directly with a small boudoir-bedroom and bath; the door by which O entered gave Anne-Marie complete freedom to come and go as she pleased. As was the case for the house they had occupied in Sannois, which opened directly onto the garden, both Anne-Marie's bedroom and sitting room opened onto the park. The grounds were cool and empty, filled with tall, stately trees as yet untouched by the approaching autumn, whereas the ivy covering the walls had already begun to turn red. Standing in the middle of the living room, O looked around at the white woodwork, the Directory-style rustic furniture made of light wood, and the large sofa in an alcove, like the easy chairs upholstered with a blue-and-yellow-striped material. The floor was covered with a blue wall-to-wall carpet. The French doors were curtained with long drapes of blue taffeta.

'You're daydreaming, O,' Anne-Marie said suddenly. 'What are you waiting for to go and get undressed? I'll send someone to fetch your things and bring you whatever you need. And when you're naked I want you to come over here.'

Handbag, gloves, jacket, sweater, skirt, garter

belt, stockings: O put them all on the same armchair near the door, and put her shoes under the chair. Then she walked over to Anne-Marie who, after having rung the bell next to the fireplace once, then again, had sat down on the sofa.

'Why O, your little lips are clearly visible now that you're clean-shaven,' Anne-Marie exclaimed as she gently parted them. 'I didn't realize that you had such a prominent mound, or that you were so highly slit . . .'

'But everyone . . .,' O protested.

'No, my dear love, *not* everyone!'

And, without letting go of O, she turned to a tall brunette who had just entered the room, doubtless in response to Anne-Marie's rings, and added:

'Look, Monique, this is the girl I branded last summer for Sir Stephen. It's very well done, isn't it? Here, feel.'

O felt Monique's hand, cool and light, gently probing the hollows of the initials engraved in her buttocks. Then the hand slipped between her thighs and grasped the disk that was suspended from her nether lips.

'So she's pierced too?' Monique said.

'Of course, he had me pierce her and affix the disk,' Anne-Marie responded, and her answer suddenly made O wonder whether her 'of course' meant that Anne-Marie found it perfectly natural to do so, or whether it was customary for Sir Stephen to both brand and pierce. In that case, should she conclude that he had done it to others before her? She heard herself, amazed, as the words struck her own ears, at her own audacity, asking Anne-Marie that last question, and was even more amazed to hear Anne-Marie answer her by saying:

'That's none of your business, O, but, since

you're so much in love and so jealous, I can nonetheless tell you that he hasn't. I've often enlarged and whipped other girls for him, but you're the first one I've marked for him. I do believe he loves you, for once in his life.'

Then she sent O into the bathroom, telling her to bathe and freshen up while Monique was off fetching her a collar and wrist bracelets.

O began to draw her bath, removed her makeup, brushed her hair, stepped into the bathtub, and, once immersed in the refreshing warmth, began slowly to soap herself. She paid no attention to what she was doing, letting her mind wander as she tried to picture, with a mixture of curiosity and pleasure, the girls who, before her, had caught Sir Stephen's fancy. Curiosity: she would have liked to know them. She was not really surprised that he had had all of them enlarged and whipped, but she was nonetheless jealous that there had been others before her, that she had not been the first for him. Standing up in the bathtub, bent over with her back to the mirror that covered the wall, she gently soaped her buttocks and the inside of her thighs, then rinsed herself to remove the suds and shifted her buttocks to look at herself in the mirror: that is what she would have liked to see, the other girls in just such a pose. How long had he kept them? So she had not been mistaken when she had had the feeling that others before had followed—naked and submissive and in a state of fear and trembling—Sir Stephen's faithful old retainer Norah. But that she had been the only one to bear his irons and the mark on her buttocks overwhelmed her with a feeling of happiness.

She stepped out of the water and began to dry herself. She heard Anne-Marie's voice through the bathroom door, calling her.

63

On Anne-Marie's bed, which was covered with a hand-embroidered purple and white percale counterpane, identical to the double drapes that framed the window, there was a pile of long dresses, corsets, mules with high heels, and the strongbox which contained the wrist bracelets. Anne-Marie, who was seated on the foot of the bed, made O kneel down in front of her, then took from one of her trouser pockets the flat key which unlocked the collars and bracelets and which she kept attached to her belt by a long thin chain. She tried a number of collars on O, until she found one that, without choking her, fit her snugly enough half way up the neck so that it was difficult to turn it in one direction or the other and yet it was even more difficult to insert a finger between the metal and the neck itself. The same applied to her wrists, to which the bracelets were fastened just above the pulse, which was left unencumbered.

The collar and bracelets that O had worn herself and seen others wear the previous year had been of leather, and had been worn much more tightly. These were of stainless steel, made in such a way as to be slightly flexible like certain wrist-watch bands. They were about two inches wide, and each had a ring of the same metal. Never had the leather accouterments of the previous year felt so cold, nor had they given O such a strong impression of being so irrevocably in chains. The metal was the same color and the same dull finish as the irons attached to her nether lips. Anne-Marie said to her, her words coinciding with the final click of the closing collar, that she would never remove either collar or bracelets, day or night, not even when she bathed, during her entire stay at Roissy.

O got to her feet, and Monique took her by the hand and led her over in front of a full-length, three-sided mirror where she applied a light red, slightly liquid lipstick to her lips with a tiny brush: O noted that the color darkened as it dried. With the same red, she painted her nipples, including the tips, and then the tiny lips between her thighs, emphasizing the upper reaches of the slit. O never learned what product she used, but it was more some kind of dye than makeup: it did not come off when it was rubbed, and even when she was removing her makeup, using alcohol, it only came off with considerable difficulty. After she had thus been made up, she was allowed to powder her face and choose a pair of mules that fit. But when she went to take one of the vaporizers on the dressing table Anne-Marie exclaimed:

'Have you lost your mind? Why in the world do you think Monique has just finished making you up? You know as well as I do that now that you're wearing all your irons you don't have the right to touch yourself.'

Then Anne-Marie herself took the vaporizer and, in the mirror, O saw her breasts and armpits gleam beneath the welter of droplets, as though they were covered with perspiration. Then Anne-Marie led her back over to the dressing-table bench and told her to raise and spread her thighs which Monique, holding her by the back of the legs, kept spread. And the fine spray of perfume that inundated the hollows between her thighs and her buttocks burned her so that she moaned and struggled.

'Hold her until it's dry,' Anne-Marie said, 'then find a corset for her.'

O was surprised at how happy she was to find herself once again ensconced in the tight-fitting black corset. She had obeyed and inhaled deeply to pull in her waist and stomach when Anne-

Marie had told her to, while Monique tightened the laces. The corset came up to beneath her breasts, which an unobtrusive vertical stay kept separated and a narrow horizontal stay supported so firmly that they were projected forward, and seemed all the more fragile and free.

'Your breasts are really made for the riding crop, O,' Anne-Marie noted. 'Do you realize that?'

'I know,' O said, 'but please, I beg you . . .'

Anne-Marie burst out laughing.

'Oh, don't worry, I'm not the one who makes that kind of decision,' she said. 'But if any of the customers should want to whip you, you can protest and beg until you're blue in the face.'

Without being fully aware of it, the word 'customer,' far more than the feeling of terror which she felt at the thought of the whip, overwhelmed O. Why 'customers'? But she did not have time to pursue the questioning any further, so struck was she, again without consciously realizing it, by what Anne-Marie told her a minute later. O was, therefore, standing in front of the mirror, with her mules on her feet and her waist throttled by her corset. Monique came over to her, carrying over her arm a skirt and blouse of yellow faille embroidered with a gray floral design.

'No, no, not that,' Monique exclaimed. 'Her uniform first.'

'What uniform?' O asked.

'The same one that Monique is wearing. Look for yourself,' Anne-Marie said.

Monique was wearing a dress cut roughly the same as the long dresses that O remembered, but Monique's was more severe, more staid, an effect which doubtless stemmed from the material—a very dark gray-blue wool—and the shawl which covered her head, shoulders, and bosom. When O

66

had donned the same clothing and saw herself in the mirror beside Monique, she realized what it was that had surprised her when she had seen Monique. It was an outfit which oddly resembled those worn in women's prisons, or by servants in convents. But not if you really looked closely at them. The wide, full skirt, lined with taffeta of the same color, was sewed onto a band with large, open, unpressed pleats that fastened over the corset, exactly like certain evening gowns do. And although it appeared closed, it was open in the middle of the back from the waistline down to the feet. Unless you deliberately pulled the dress to one side or the other, however, you would never have noticed it. O noticed it on hers only after they had put on her skirt, and she had failed to remark it earlier on Monique's. The blouse, which buttoned in the back, had short, scalloped peplums which covered, for about the width of a person's hand, the onset of the pleats. It was fitted with darts and two elastic panels. The sleeves were cut out but not sewed on, with a seam on the upper part of the arm that extended to the shoulder seam and ended at the elbow in a wide, flared bias. A similar bias piped the décolleté neckline which tightly followed the curve of the corset. But a large scarf of black lace covered her head, one corner of which hung down in the middle of her forehead, like a kerchief, while the other corner extended down her back, falling between her shoulder blades. It was fastened by four snaps, two on the shoulder seams and two on the bias of the low-cut neckline, just at the rise of the breasts, and crossed between them, where a long steel pin held it taut to the corset. The lace, held in the hair by a comb, framed the face and completely concealed the breasts, but was supple and transparent enough so that you could make out the nipples, as you knew that the breasts were free beneath the shawl. Besides, all you had to do to make them completely bare was to remove the pin, as, in the back, all you had to do was spread the two folds of the skirt to bare the backside.

Before she undressed her again, Monique showed O how, with two straps that raised the two sections of the skirt and then tied in front at the waist, it was a simple matter to keep them open. It was while she was demonstrating this that, in effect, Anne-Marie answered the question raised by O:

'It's the uniform of the community,' she said. 'You didn't have a chance to get acquainted with it on your last visit because then you were brought here by your lover for his own account. You were not, properly speaking, a member of the community.'

'But I don't understand,' said O. 'I was just like the other girls. Anyone could . . .'

'Anyone could sleep with you? Of course they could. But it was for your lover's pleasure, and the only person it concerned was he. Now it's different. Sir Stephen has turned you over to the community. Everyone can still sleep with you, true, but now it's the community's problem. You'll be paid . . .'

'Paid!' O exclaimed. 'But Sir Stephen . . .'

Anne-Marie did not let her finish.

'Listen, O, I've heard quite enough. If Sir Stephen wants you to go to bed for money, he's certainly free to do so. It's no concern of yours. Go to bed and keep quiet. As for your other duties and obligations, we use the sister system here. Noelle will be your sister, and she'll explain all the procedures to you.'

VII

The luncheon in Anne-Marie's bedroom was a strange affair. A servant had brought the meal in on a heated serving table. Monique, in her community uniform, had served them, after having set four places at the table: Anne-Marie's, O's, Noelle's, and her own. Before lunch, O had tried on several more dresses. Anne-Marie had chosen, and put aside, the gray and yellow dress, which O would wear that same day; another blue dress; a third which was a paler blue mixed with green; and, lastly, a very tight-fitting knitted dress which opened in front from the waist down. It was dark purple, and O's pale thighs and loins, so naked and so weighted with their metal rings, were visible even when she did not move, as were her naked breasts. The servant had taken all the dresses, except the yellow one that Anne-Marie had chosen, into O's room, which adjoined Noelle's. Monique would take all the others back to the storeroom.

O watched Noelle, who was seated opposite her, laughing. She was laughing because the black horsehair of the chair on which she was sitting tickled her; O glanced over at Anne-Marie, who was trying to control her temper but was on the verge of losing it, then at Monique, who was concentrating on her domestic table duties. On two occasions, when Monique got up from her place, O saw Anne-Marie, as Monique passed to her right, slip her hand into the slit in Monique's dress. Monique froze, and O realized, or rather guessed, from the slight yielding of her body, that she was accommodating herself to the probing hand.

'Why didn't he say anything to me about it?' O kept repeating to herself, over and over. 'Why didn't he?'

And sometimes she had the feeling that, quite simply, she had been abandoned, and that Sir Stephen had sent her to Roissy, turned her over to Roissy, as Anne-Marie had put it, in order to get rid of her. And then again she imagined that the opposite was true, that he had done it because he desired her all the more. Then Anne-Marie was right: whatever he wanted was of no concern of hers, nor were his reasons any of her business; all that mattered was that he had his own good reasons. And at that point the whole cycle would begin all over again: 'Why didn't he say anything to me? Why didn't he?' And what could she do, at this juncture, to keep the tears from flowing, or at least to keep the others from seeing them flow? Noelle saw them. She gave her a slight but very tender smile and shook her finger at her, signifying that O ought to control herself. O smiled in return and dried her eyes with both her fists, the way children do when they've been scolded. She didn't have any napkin, and she was naked. Luckily, Anne-Marie, who had removed the pin holding Monique's scarf and was busy caressing the brownish tips of her breasts, was not looking at O. She was watching Monique's face to see the nascent signs of pleasure reflected there, and even while she caressed she kept plying her with questions: How many men had entered her body since the previous evening? Who were they? Had she been as open to them as she was now?

As she said these last words, Anne-Marie called Noelle and O, and, without letting go of Monique, had them lift and fasten the two sides of her dress. Monique had generous, golden buttocks, and finely shaped, unmarked thighs. In a monotone, Monique had answered each of Anne-Marie's questions: Five men had taken her, three of whom she did not know; she gave the names of the other two. Yes, she had opened herself as best she could. Anne-Marie, making Monique bend over, demonstrated to the other two girls how easily she was able to plunge, one after the other, the two longest fingers of her hand first into the sex then into the rear. Each time she did they could see Monique's buttocks contract as she closed around the fingers, moaning. Finally she gave a cry, her hands gripped her breasts, her head was thrown back, and, beneath her black veil, her eyes closed. Anne-Marie let her go.

It was not until after midnight that O, the evening of that first day, was taken and chained in her room. She had spent the afternoon in the library, dressed in her lovely gray and yellow dress lined with matching yellow taffeta, whose voluminous folds she took in both her hands to raise whenever the order was given to her to lift her skirt. Noelle, who was dressed in a similar red dress, was with her as were two blonde girls, whose names Noelle failed to tell her until they were alone that evening: the rule of silence, in the presence of any male, were he a master or a valet, was absolute.

It was just three o'clock in the afternoon when the four girls entered the empty room, whose windows were wide open. It was warm and pleasant; the sun struck the wall of the main building at right angles, its reflection casting a false light on one of the ivy-covered walls. And O was mistaken. The room was not empty: there was a valet standing on guard duty against a door. O knew that she had no right to look at him, but she couldn't help doing so. Being careful not to raise her eyes any higher than the man's waist, she found herself once again overwhelmed with the same feeling of panic and fascination which she had experienced a year earlier. No, she had forgotten nothing, and yet, in actuality, it was worse than in her memory, this sex so free in its pouch, and so visible between the thighs of the tight-fitting black breeches like those one sees in sixteenth-century paintings— and the thongs of the whip he kept stuck in his belt. At the foot of the easy chairs there were stools, and O, following the example of the other three girls, sat down on one of them with her dress spread out in a broad arc around her. And it was from this lowly position that O looked up at this statuesque, unmoving man standing directly opposite her. The silence was so heavy you could have cut it with a knife, and O was afraid even to shift the folds of her dress: the crackling of the silk would have been too loud. She gave a cry at the sudden sound that broke that silence. A swarthy, thickset young man in a riding outfit, a riding crop in one hand, his boots adorned with golden spurs, had entered the room by straddling the windowsill.

'What a pretty picture,' he said. 'As sensible as you are well mannered. But what are you doing here all alone? Is there no one here to appreciate your charms? I've been watching you through the window for a good fifteen minutes. But the beauty in yellow,' he added, running the tip of his riding crop over O's breasts, 'yes, you,' he said, 'you haven't been as well mannered as the others, have you?'

74

O got to her feet. Just as she did, Monique came into the room, her purple satin dress tucked up in front at her waist, beneath which a triangle of dark fleece marked the beginning of her long thighs which O had previously seen only from the rear. She was followed by two men. O recognized the first. He was the one who, the previous year, had outlined to her the rules that governed at Roissy. He recognized her too and smiled at her.

'Do you know her?' the young man who had preceded them into the room wanted to know.

'Yes,' the man said. 'Her name is O. She is marked by Sir Stephen, who took her over from René R. She was here for a few weeks last year, when you were away. If you'd like, Frank . . .'

'You know, I just might,' said Frank. 'But do you realize what your O's been doing? For the past fifteen minutes I've been watching her without her being aware of it, and during the entire time she was staring at José, but not above his waist.'

The three men laughed. Frank took O by the nipples and pulled her toward him.

'Tell me the truth, my little whore, what was it you were staring at with such desire, José's whip, or his prick?'

O, flushed and burning with shame, losing all notion of what was allowed and what was forbidden at Roissy, tore herself loose from the young man's grasp, jumping back and screaming, 'Leave me alone! Leave me alone!'

He caught her as she stumbled over an easy chair and brought her back to her former position.

'You're wrong to try and run away,' he said. 'The whip. José is going to give it to you before you know it.'

Ah, if only she could keep herself from moaning,

from grovelling and begging for mercy! But she did moan and cry and ask to be spared, she twisted and turned trying to get away from the rain of blows, she tried to kiss Frank's hands, the hands that were holding her while the valet flogged away. One of the blonde girls, together with Noelle, helped her to her feet and straightened out her skirt.

'Now I'm taking her,' said Frank. 'I'll let you have my opinion shortly.'

But when she had followed him into his room and was naked in his bed, before he lay down beside her he said:

'I'm sorry, O, but your lover also has you whipped, doesn't he?'

'Yes,' O said, then hesitated, as though she had intended to say more but had thought better of it.

'Go on,' he said. 'Speak your mind.'

'He doesn't insult me,' O said.

'Are you quite sure he doesn't?' Frank said. 'He's never called you a whore?'

O shook her head, and even as she did she realized that she was lying. Whore was indeed what Sir Stephen had called her when he had taken her to the Laperouse restaurant and given her to the two Englishmen, when he had stripped her naked during the meal, her breasts crisscrossed with scars. She raised her eyes until they met Frank's eyes, staring fixedly at her. They were dark blue, gentle, almost compassionate; he had realized that she was lying when she had told him that her lover had never called her a whore.

Responding to his unspoken words, she murmured:

'If he does, it's with good reason.'

He kissed her on the mouth.

'Do you really love him all that much?' he said.

'Yes,' O said.

That seemed to close the conversation, or at least Frank did not feel like pursuing it any further. He caressed her, with his lips, so long and tenderly in the hollow of her thighs that her breathing came faster and deeper until she could no longer control it. When after having penetrated deep inside he shifted position and entered her from behind, he called her, in a near whisper: 'O.' O felt herself tightening around the pale of flesh that filled and burned her. He lost himself within her and quickly fell asleep, snuggled against her, with his hands on her breasts and his knees pressed tightly against the hollows of her knees.

It was cool. O pulled the sheet and blanket up over them and fell asleep too. The day was drawing to a close when they awoke. How many months had it been since O had last slept for so long in a man's arms? All of them, first and foremost Sir Stephen, slept with her, then left her, or sent her away. And this one, who only a short while before had treated her so coarsely, so churlishly, was now seated at her feet, asking her jokingly, like Hamlet to Ophelia (Ophelia because of 'O,' he said), whether he could curl up and sleep in her lap. With his head against O's upper thighs and belly, he toyed with her irons, turning them over and over. He lighted a lamp the better to see them, read out loud the name of Sir Stephen inscribed on the disk, and then, remarking on the crossed whip and riding crop engraved beneath the name, asked O which Sir Stephen preferred to use, the whip or the crop. O did not reply.

'Come on, answer me, child,' he said tenderly.

'I don't know,' O said. 'Both, I guess. But with Norah it was always the whip.'

'Who's Norah?'

He spoke so unreservedly, in such a candid and trusting manner, he gave such an impression that it was prefectly natural for her to be answering him, that it was as though she were answering herself, as though she were talking to herself out loud, that O replied without even giving it a second thought.

'His maid,' she said.

'So I did well to have José whip you.'

'Yes,' O said.

'And what about him,' the young man went on. 'What does he prefer to have you do to him?'

He waited, but this time O failed to respond to his question.

'I know,' he said. 'I want you to do the same to me, O: caress me with your mouth.'

And he raised himself till he was over her, and she caressed him. Then with both hands he took her by the waist, to help her to her feet, saying: 'Slender, how very slender!' then kissed her breasts and laced up her corset. O let him do whatever he wanted without even thanking him, overwhelmed with a feeling of gentleness and comfort, like some tamed creature. He was talking to her about Sir Stephen. When he said to her, before he rang for a servant to take her back to her quarters, after she had put her dress back on: 'Tomorrow I'll send for you again, O, but next time I'll whip you myself,' she smiled because he added: 'I'll whip you the way he does.'

VIII

O was later to learn from Noelle, that evening in fact, that if the valets were forbidden to touch the girls in any of the common rooms, with exception of the refectory, where their word was law, they were free to do with them as they pleased wherever their duties called them (but only there): in the girls' quarters when they were there alone, in the dressing rooms, and even in the hallways and lobbies. As chance would have it, the person who answered Frank's ring was José. He was young, tall, and very well built. The naturally arrogant air of Spanish men was becoming to his Moorish face. Once again O was overwhelmed with a feeling of shame as she followed him, with her mules clacking noisily, down the long hallway. It was not because he had flogged her, but because she was sure he had believed what Frank had said to him, and that he was firmly convinced that O desired him. And she could not rid herself of the memory of what some colonial officer had said to her about the Spanish soldiers of North African descent: whenever they could, they spent the entire day in the saddle.

José had not taken ten steps when he indeed turned around and, having come abreast of the first bench along the hallway, which he pushed against the wall to make things easier, grabbed O and threw her down on it. He took her slowly, leisurely, and O, furious with herself, but being worked over by an iron bar as a field by a persistent plow, was unable to prevent herself from moaning with pleasure.

'You enjoying it?' he asked her. 'You like it?' the second 'it' not referring to the act itself but to the instrument he was wielding.

His white teeth gleamed in his swarthy face. O closed her eyes so that she would not have to see his smile. But he bent down over her and took her tongue. Why was O so afraid she could feel herself trembling at the idea that Frank's door might open?

In the ground floor bathroom, where José then took her, O found Noelle, who was holding her skirts up while another girl in uniform, with the crossed scarf, was douching her. O squatted down in like fashion over the Turkish-style toilet next to the one Noelle was using. When she had eliminated the last drops of water from her body, the same girl who had been administering to Noelle soaped her for a moment, then rinsed her with a spray, activated by the pressure of her finger, that spouted from a round metal tube topped by an ebonite nozzle. The spray was gentle, but the water was cold, colder still, it seemed to her, than when she had felt it running into the depths of her bowels, then her vagina. Was it really necessary to douche her so meticulously and at such great length a second time, this time concentrating on the loins, the inside of the thighs, and the opening of her vagina? During her first stay at Roissy she had not even been aware that these bathrooms existed. It is also true that then she had never been in any room other than her own.

'The rule is, O,' Noelle explained to her when she later had a chance to ask her about it, 'that each time we go upstairs we're sent down for a douche afterward.'

'But why for such a long time,' said O, 'and why so cold?'

'Personally, I like it,' Noelle said. 'You feel so cool and fresh afterward, and so nicely contracted.'

The girl on duty then gave them both some lipstick and perfume. They made themselves up and both brushed their hair. The perfume warmed O slightly. Noelle took her by the hand. She was lovely, with that Irish type of beauty you also find in certain parts of Brittany, with black hair, very white skin, and blue eyes. She was no taller than O, but she had narrow shoulders, a relatively small head, tiny pointed breasts, and generous, well-rounded hips. Her small pert nose and full lips, which were always half-parted, gave her a saucy, laughing air. But it was also a fact that she was generally good humored: whenever she entered a room, one always had the impression that she was coming to a party. There was something disarming about her cheerfulness. She lent herself to anyone's command or desire with such a charming smile, she lifted her skirts so readily, revealing the lovely expanse of her white buttocks, that it was rare indeed that she was seriously whipped. 'Just enough, no more and no less,' she used to say to O, 'but the fact of the matter is I don't look good all marked up.'

When they entered the main salon, O had a chance to admire Noelle's gracefulness, and the success that she garnered as a result of that charm. The three men seated in the big leather armchairs, two of whom had a fair-haired girl seated at their feet, while Monique was seated at the feet of the third, paid no attention to any of

the three—one of the blondes was a girl named
Madeleine whom O recognized from her visit to
Roissy the year before—but turned their heads
and greeted Noelle. One of them called to her
immediately, saying:

'Come over here and give me your pretty
breasts.'

Noelle complied, leaning over the chair with
her hands on the arms, her breasts at the level of
the man's mouth; she did so without the slightest
hesitation, obviously happy to please him. He
was a man of about forty, bald and ruddy-
complexioned—O could see his red neck which
formed two little folds of fat just above the collar
of his jacket—who reminded her of the pseudo-
German to whom Sir Stephen had given her the
evening before; he did in fact resemble him.

The man who was with Monique moved over
until he was behind Noelle, and ran one of his
hands over her buttocks.

'Do you mind, Pierre?' he asked the first man.

'Don't ask me, ask Noelle for permission,' he
responded, then added: 'But that really isn't
necessary, is it Noelle?'

'No,' Noelle said.

O looked at her: she was ravishing, with her
neck and head thrown back the better to offer her
breasts, and arching her back the better to offer
her buttocks. Was it her own pleasure, the obvious
pleasure that she herself derived at seeing herself
the object of their eyes and their caresses, that
aroused desire in others? Monique's companion
had made a sign to her to unbutton him, and O
watched him grow erect between Noelle's thighs.
Finally, all three men possessed her one after the
other, rose and black in the hollow of her thighs,
all blooming and white as snow in her swirling red
dress.

And it was she, immediately thereafter, and O—the latter because, as Pierre put it, 'Let's send the child, since she's with her'—whom they unanimously picked out when a valet arrived to ask whether they could spare two girls who were needed in the bar.

'If she doesn't get cracking soon,' said Pierre, 'she'll be rusty from lack of practice.'

IX

At Roissy, there were three gates. The part of the building to which one could not gain access without passing through one of these three gates constituted what was called, not without some degree of childish playfulness, the main enclosure. The only ones who were permitted access to it were the associates or, more simply, the members of the Club. This closed-in area consisted of—on the ground floor, to the right of a large vestibule (onto which one of the gates, the largest, opened)—the library, a sitting room, a smoking room, a dressing room-bathroom; and to the left, the girls' refectory and an adjoining room which served as the valets' dormitory. A few rooms on the ground floor were occupied by the girls that members of the Club brought there, as O had been brought the previous year by René. The other rooms on the floors above were occupied by Club members who were spending a short or longer period of time at Roissy. Within the confines of the restricted area the girls were only allowed to come and go accompanied by someone else; they were absolutely bound to the rule of silence, even among themselves, and to keeping their eyes lowered at all times; at all times, too, they were obliged to be bare-breasted, and more often than not to keep their skirts hoisted either in front or behind. One could do

89

with them as one desired. No matter what a member did with them, no matter what demands he made upon them, the price was the same. A member could come three times a year or three times a week, stay for an hour or for a fortnight, simply have a girl strip for him or flog her till she was bleeding, the cost of the annual membership was exactly the same. The cost of a member's stay at Roissy was calculated the way it would have been at any hotel.

The second gate separated this central part of the building from a wing they called the little enclosure. It was in the extension of this wing that Anne-Marie lived, and it was here, too, that the girls who actually lived in the community had their quarters. These girls, who belonged as it were to Roissy, were lodged in double rooms, in that each room was divided by a semi-partition against which, on either side, the beds were placed back to back. They were ordinary beds, and not the furcovered sofa which had graced the room where O had stayed on her first visit. The girls shared a bathroom, as they did a closet. The doors to their rooms could not be locked, and the members of the Club could enter them any time in the course of the night, during which the girls were chained. But aside from this rule by which they were obliged to spend the night in chains, there was no other basic restriction.

Finally, on the other side of the third gate, which, as you faced the main gate, was to the left, the second gate being situated to the right, was located the free and as it were quasi-public area of Roissy: a restaurant, a bar, small sitting rooms on the ground floor, with, on the floors above, the bedrooms. The members of the Club were free to invite guests to the restaurant and bar without having to pay any entrance fee. But anyone, or virtually anyone, could purchase a 'temporary membership' whch was very expensive but gave him the right to two visits. The only rights it gave him, in effect, as guests of members were allowed to use the bar, were to have lunch or dinner in the restaurant, to rent a room, and to use it with a girl of his choice. Each of the above items was payable separately. For the bar and restaurant there were a *maitre d'hôtel* and a few waiters—the kitchens were in the basement—but it was the girls who waited on table. In the restaurant they were in uniform. In the bar, dressed in long silk dresses with a lace mantilla similar to the uniform scarf covering their hair, their shoulders, and their breasts, they were there waiting to be picked by a member or a guest. The restaurant and bar, as well as the hotel, were financially independent, their income covering their costs. The money earned by the girls was divided according to fixed percentages: so much for Roissy, so much for the girl. Nor were all the girls paid on an equal basis: O learned that she would be paid double the base rate because she officially belonged to a member of the Club, and because she wore irons and bore a brand. Two other girls were in the same category as she, one of whom was the buxom, ivory-complexioned redhead she had seen in Anne-Marie's quarters. If anyone chose to whip a girl, or have her whipped by one of the valets, there was a supplementary payment. The checks were paid at the hotel office; the tips were given directly to the personnel involved.

Its close proximity to Paris, its princely yet discreet atmosphere, the impressive buildings and park, the comfort of the installation, the excellence of the restaurant, the theatrical aspect which the costumed girls and the omnipresent

valets gave to the place, the combination of freedom and security in any and all relationships, and
last but not least the clear knowledge of what took
place behind the gates, within the confines of the
enclosure, provided Roissy with a large clientele,
made up primarily of businessmen, a goodly per-
centage of whom, at least half, were foreigners.
The public part of Roissy had no more official
existence than did the clandestine part. The term
'Country Club' fooled no one, but it often happened that the grizzled man who was thought to
be the Master of Roissy, but who in reality was
only the administrator, questioned one or the
other girl about some short-time customer—not
to mention the fact that, in order to receive one of
the temporary membership cards, the applicant
had to show his passport or some other identifica-
tion (it being made clear to him that no record was
kept at Roissy of any such papers used by the customer); in short, Roissy was officially ignored and
unofficially tolerated. One of the reasons for this,
in addition to the above-named precautions that
the establishment itself took, was doubtless that
there had never been any complaints from Roissy
about venereal disease, nor had there been any
scandal relative to pregnancies or abortions. O
had always wondered how it was possible for girls
who sometimes slept with as many as ten men a
day—men who were extremely demanding and
would put up with no show of reluctance or
embarrassment—how it was possible for them to
avoid getting pregnant. They couldn't all be
lucky, as was O: she had a physical anomaly
that practically eliminated any possibility of
pregnancy.

   'Luck?' said Anne-Marie. 'Chance? There are
ways of replacing these, O,' was the reply to O's
query on the matter.

From her answer, O came to the conclusion that Anne-Marie, who was a doctor, had secretly operated on the girls at Roissy. You never saw on any of their faces that anxious or worried look that, with other women, revealed that she was late with her period.

'Oh, it's nothing at all, really,' Noelle said to her one day, 'and afterward you never think or worry about it again. But I can't explain exactly what it is. They put me to sleep.'

But O conjectured that it was less the fact of being under anesthesia that kept her from telling more than that she had been strictly forbidden to talk about the operation.

As far as venereal disease was concerned, the matter was not so simple: the precautions they used included pills you let dissolve internally, prophylactics, and douches. The worst source of contagion was the mouth. The liquid lipstick that had been applied to her upon her arrival helped to prevent chafing and cracking, and thus to reduce the danger. And, too, Anne-Marie examined the girls daily. And if contagion did occur, they treated or, if it became necessary, isolated the girl—there were rooms directly above Anne-Marie's quarters—until she was cured.

These restrictions, and this care, did not apply to girls who were brought to Roissy by their lovers: they were strictly on their own, and what is more they never entered the main enclosure. As for the others, who or what determined how each girl was to be utilized within the confines of the restricted area and how she was to be used outside, O was never really able to figure out. There was, however, a clearly established routine for the girls when they were in uniform: so many days serving in the restaurant for lunch, so many days on duty there for dinner; similarly, when they were in their formal gowns, so many after-noons and so many evenings per week on duty in the bar. Nonetheless, since both the restaurant and the bar were open to visitors and Club members alike, there was nothing to prevent the latter from choosing a girl and taking her back behind the gates of the enclosure. As for the rest of their routine, it seemed to be a matter of caprice: for example, when the valet had come to ask for two girls for the bar, the fact that Noelle and O had been chosen rather than Monique or Madeleine.

When O entered the bar for the first time, fol-lowing close on the heels of Noelle, she was struck by its resemblance to the library they had just left: it was the same size room with the same kind of woodwork and the same easy chairs. The pretty little redhead who was shaved and bore the same kind of irons as O, and whom O had once whipped at Anne-Marie's, an experience from which she had derived, after her initial hesita-tions, a pleasure that had surprised her, was seated on a bar stool. She was dressed in gray satin and was laughing and clearly enjoying her-self with two men. As soon as she saw O she jumped off her stool, came over and kissed O, and taking her around the waist led her back over to the men with whom she had been sitting.

'I'd like you to meet O,' she said. 'Do you mind if she joins us? You won't find anyone any better.'

So saying, she kissed the tip of one of O's breasts through the black lacework covering it.

'They won't tell me their names,' she said. 'But they look nice, don't they?'

Nice was hardly the term, thought O. In fact it was absurd as applied to them. They looked both embarrassed and vulgar, and their third drink had failed to provide them with any degree of self-assurance. As O reached for her drink on the

94

bar, her arm grazed the knee of the man on her right. He put his hand on her arching bracelet and asked why they all wore iron bracelets.

'As if they didn't know!' Yvonne exclaimed. 'Never mind, we'll explain to them during dinner. Come on, let's sit down.'

Then, glancing at the man who had asked the question about the bracelets, who was getting down off his barstool, Yvonne said to O, as she herself made a point of doing the same to the other man:

'Quickly, O, touch him with your hand. Then let him try and tell you he doesn't like you.'

In the restaurant, they took a table for four. The three men who had earlier taken Noelle in the library were dining together at a neighboring table. As for Noelle, she had left the bar five minutes after O had joined Yvonne, going out the door that led to the bedrooms, followed by a rather corpulent, Middle-Eastern looking type.

Frank came into the restaurant just as they were finishing dinner. Neither O nor Yvonne had ordered an after-dinner drink, but they were waiting patiently for the men to finish their cognac. Frank made a discreet sign to O, then went over and sat down by himself at a table by the window. But O, who was seated in such a way that she had a good the slit in her skirt. In the restaurant or bar, this was the only liberty allowed, and even then on condition it was done discreetly.

Finally, the time came when Yvonne said:

'Shall we go upstairs?'

One of the hotel waiters showed them to two adjoining, but noncommunicating, rooms; he indicated where the telephone was, the bell for service, then shut the door behind him as he left.

O, without even being asked, removed her mantilla and went over to her customer to offer him her breasts. He was seated on a chair. The three-sided mirror which graced one of the walls of every room reflected him, and O, standing between his legs and leaning over in order to make it easier for him, was nonetheless slightly astonished to find how natural it was for her to offer her breasts to this unknown man. Since that morning, four different men had, as Anne-Marie put it, entered her body: Sir Stephen, the driver, Frank, and José. This man would be the fifth, which would bring her even with Monique. But this one would pay her. He told her to get undressed, and when he saw her encorseted, he stopped her. Her irons (about which Yvonne had not said a word, whereas she had offered, gratuitously, long after either of the men had thought of querying her further about the wrist bracelets: 'Our bracelets are so that we can be tied up whenever anyone wants to whip us') made a profound impression on him, as did view of him, from a slight angle, noticed that as soon as the girl who was scheduled to wait on him approached his table he had slipped his hand into the double opening which was offered to him when he held her by her hams sprawled back on the edge of the bed. No sooner had he emerged from her than he said:

'If you're really good, I'll give you a fat tip.'

She got down on her knees.

He left before she was dressed, leaving a handful of banknotes on the mantel of the fireplace: about a third as much as O earned in a month in the photo studio on the rue Royale. She washed herself, put on her dress, and went back downstairs, after having neatly folded the banknotes and stuffed them into her cleavage.

The truth of the matter was that she was mistaken when she figured she would end up with the same body count as Monique at the end of the day. As soon as she went into the bar, another customer picked her and took her back up to one of the rooms, where he possessed her, making her total for the day not five but six.

X

In the dark, chained to the hook above her bed—as she had been in her room the previous year, in that room now occupied by someone else, she had no idea who—in the dark and unable to sleep, O asked herself for the hundredth time why, whether or not she derived any pleasure from it, someone, no matter whom, from the fact that he penetrated her, or simply opened her with his hand, beat her or only made her strip naked, had the power to make her submit to his will.

On the other side of the partition, which was only as long as the width of the bed and the night tables and no thicker than a screen, she heard Noelle stirring, and realized that she too was unable to fall asleep. She called to her. Did Noelle feel as subjugated, as submissive as she? Did she feel as mastered, as servile as O did the minute someone touched her? Noelle was indignant. Submissive? Servile? She did what had to be done, and that was the long and the short of it. And mastered? Why mastered? O was indeed a very complicated young lady. Noelle found it flattering to see men stiffening in her presence, because of her; she found it amusing to open her legs or her mouth to them.

'Even to that Syrian, or whatever he was, you went with tonight?' said O.

'What Syrian?' Noelle wanted to know.

'That dark man with the frizzy hair, the big pot-bellied man you went upstairs with right after we got to the bar.' And as she said it she thought to herself, So that's how it is; after awhile you can't even remember. But she did remember.

'Oh, him!' said Noelle. 'You should have seen him naked. A big fat pig.'

'That's exactly what I mean,' O said.

'But you're wrong,' Noelle protested. 'What difference does it make? He tongued me for at least half an hour, but what he really wanted was to take me from the rear. With me on all fours, of course. He pays very well, you know.'

O had also been paid very well. The money was right there, in the drawer of one of the night tables.

'Noelle,' O said, 'tell me honestly, when they whip you, do you really enjoy it?'

'A little; but the truth is they only whip me a little.'

O almost said: 'You're lucky,' then she realized that it had nothing whatever to do with luck. She was about to ask Noelle why it was they never whipped her more than 'a little,' and what she thought of chains, and her opinion on the valets ... But Noelle turned over in her bed and whimpered:

'Oh, I'm so tired I can't keep my eyes open another minute. For goodness' sake, O, stop fretting and thinking so much, and go to sleep.'

So O bit her tongue and said no more.

XI

In the morning, at ten o'clock, a valet came to undo the chains. After the bath, the morning ablutions, and Anne-Marie's medical inspection, the girls—unless they were on duty in the rooms of the main enclosure, in which case they had to immediately don their uniforms—were free to get dressed or not, until it was time to go down either to the restaurant or bar, if it was their turn to serve there, or to the refectory if it was not. But those who went to the refectory did not get dressed. Why should they, since they were supposed to be naked while there? There was a room on the floor where they could go for breakfast. The doors to the girls' bedrooms remained open, and they were allowed to visit one another freely. Only O, Yvonne, and the third girl, Julienne, who were branded and wore irons, were summoned in the morning to be whipped. The whipping was administered to each of them in turn on the stairway landing of their floor. The balustrade was used as the whipping post, over which, after they had been tied, they were made to lean. The whipping was never severe enough to mark them, but long and hard enough to make them scream, beg for mercy, and sometimes cry. The first morning that O, after she was untied, returned to her room and collapsed on her bed, still moaning from the burning pain in her loins, Noelle took her in her arms to comfort her. Her kindness and solicitous concern were, however, tinged with contempt. Why had she ever agreed to be pierced in the first place, or allowed those rings to be inserted in her nether lips? O confessed quite candidly that she was happy she had consented to the rings, and that her lover whipped her every day.

'So you're used to it,' Noelle said. 'Then don't go around complaining. You'd probably miss it if they stopped.'

'Maybe I would,' said O. 'And I'm not complaining. But don't say I'm used to it. No, I'll never get used to it . . .'

'In that case,' Noelle said, 'you're going to really have something to complain about, because the days will be few and far between when they only whip you once here. When they see a girl like you, men know right away that you're made to be flogged. They sense it. And if they don't, the brand and the rings give it away. Not to mention that it will be on your card.'

'On my card,' said O. 'What card? What are you talking about?'

'You don't have your card yet, but don't worry, when you get it that information will be on it.'

Questioned about the card three days later when O was invited to lunch in her apartment, Anne-Marie had no hesitation about explaining what it was.

'I'm waiting for your photos,' she said. 'We'll transcribe on the back the information from the card that Sir Stephen sent me about you. I don't mean your vital statistics, your description, age, and all that, but your special characteristics, your profession, and so forth . . . Oh, it's brief enough; it will all fit on a couple of lines, and I know just what it will say.'

The photographs of O had been taken one

morning in a studio just like the one where O had once worked, which was set up under the eaves of the right wing of the building. O had been made up the way she used to make up the models, in that not-so-distant past that, nonetheless, seemed further removed from her than her earliest childhood. She had been photographed in her uniform, in her long yellow dress; she had been photographed with her dress tucked up in front and behind; she had been photographed naked, from in front, from behind, in profile; standing, lying down, half sprawling backward on a table with her legs spread wide; bent over with her buttocks sticking out; kneeling down with her hands tied. Were they going to keep all the poses?

'Yes,' Anne-Marie told her. 'They put them in your file. They make prints of the best ones and give them to the customers.'

When Anne-Marie showed them to her two days later she was thunderstruck. Not that they were not all lovely; there wasn't a single one that could not have been used in those clandestine photo magazines they sell under the counter at all the Paris kiosks. But the only one that O felt she honestly recognized herself in was a photograph taken of her full-face, standing stark naked, leaning against the edge of a table, with her hands behind her, behind her buttocks actually, with her legs slightly spread so that the irons were clearly visible between her thighs, and her lower lips as clearly defined as was her slightly parted mouth. She was staring straight ahead, as though lost in her own thoughts. She obviously was not alone in especially remarking that shot.

'That's the one they'll be giving out the most,' Anne-Marie said to her. 'You can look at the other side. No, wait, I'll show you the card Sir Stephen sent.'

She got up, opened the drawer of a writing desk, and handed O a thin card on which there appeared, in red ink in Sir Stephen's hand, her name: O, and the following notations: 'Bears irons. Branded. Very sensitive, well-trained mouth.' Below which, underlined: 'Should be whipped.'

'Give me back the photograph,' Anne-Marie said. The same information was fully transcribed on the back of the photo. What it said was nothing more or less than what Sir Stephen had said in O's presence, in less elegant terms, every time he had turned her over to someone else and even—he had never made any effort to conceal the fact from O—whenever he talked about her to his friends. O learned that two or three photographs of this kind for each girl at Roissy were in the loose-leaf album that anyone in the bar or restaurant could consult.

'That's the picture Sir Stephen prefers,' Anne-Marie said. 'That one and . . .' extracting another one from the assortment, 'this one.' The second was a pose where O was kneeling, with her skirts hoisted up.

'What do you mean?' O exclaimed. 'You mean Sir Stephen has seen them?'

'Yes, of course he has,' Anne-Marie said. 'He saw them yesterday when he was here. He made out your card while he was here, too.'

'But when, yesterday?' O wanted to know, her face ashen, feeling the lump in her throat growing and the tears rising. 'When? Why didn't he see me?'

'Oh, he saw you,' Anne-Marie said. 'I went into the library with him yesterday while you were there. You were with the Commander. You and he were the only ones in the room, but we weren't going to interrupt him.'

Yesterday, yesterday afternoon in the library, O, on her knees, her blue and green dress hoisted up over her buttocks . . . She hadn't moved when the door had opened: the Commander's member had been in her mouth.

'Why are you crying, O?' Anne-Marie went on. 'He found you very pretty. Stop crying, you little fool.'

But O could not stem the flow of tears.

'Why didn't he call me? Did he leave right after that? What did he do? Why didn't he say anything to me?' she lamented.

'Incredible!' Anne-Marie interrupted. 'Now you're making him accountable to you for what he does. I thought he had trained you better. The next time I see him I'll make sure not to congratulate him on your excellent discipline. What you deserve is . . .'

Anne-Marie broke off. Someone was knocking at her door. The person who came in was the one referred to as the Master of Roissy. Till now, he had scarcely paid any attention to O since her arrival, and had not touched her. But she was probably especially moving, or provocative, in her state of distress and disarray, sitting there pale and naked, her mouth open and trembling. As Anne-Marie ordered her back to her room to get dressed—it was almost three o'clock—he countermanded the order:

'No,' he said. 'Tell her to wait for me outside in the hallway.'

XII

In the depths of her distress, O was somewhat
soothed by a circumstance where it seemed that
nothing could be anything but unpleasant to her:
the arrival of the pseudo-German who had
already, in Sir Stephen's presence, possessed her
a number of times. To be sure, there was nothing
very pleasant about the man. He was a coarse,
churlish fellow, who gave the impression of being
greedy and supercilious. His language, as well as
his hands, could well have been those of a truck-
driver. But he said to O, in the bar where he was
waiting and to which he had had her summoned,
that he had been sent by Sir Stephen and asked
her to have dinner with him. At the same time he
handed her an envelope. O remembered, her heart
skipping a beat, the envelope that she had found
on the table in Sir Stephen's living room the day
after the first night she had spent there. She
opened it. It was indeed a word from Sir Stephen,
asking her to do her best to treat Carl in such a
way as to induce him to pay a return visit to
Roissy, as he had asked her in the course of their
return trip to Paris from the Riviera to seduce
him into following her into her compartment.
And he thanked her. Carl clearly did not know the
contents of the letter. Sir Stephen must have
implied to him that the letter contained another
message altogether.

When O put the piece of paper back into its envelope and raised her eyes to him, seated on one of the barstools (she was standing beside him), he said to her in that drawling, almost guttural voice, made even more halting by his lack of fluency in French and his thick German accent:

'So, you will be obedient?'

'Oh, yes,' said O. Yes, indeed she would be obedient! He would think it was for him. She didn't care a damn about Carl, but she did care that Sir Stephen wanted to use her for his own purpose, in whatever way he desired, and no matter what that purpose may have been!

She looked at Carl almost tenderly. If she succeeded in making him want to come back—the reasons why Sir Stephen wanted to keep him in Paris, that at least was her impression of what he wanted, interested her not in the least—if she succeeded, perhaps Sir Stephen would reward her, perhaps he would come to Roissy. She gathered the rustling folds of her dress, smiled at the German, and preceded him into the restaurant. Whether it was her gentleness, which when she made an effort was truly delightful, or her smile, O had the pleasant surprise of seeing Carl's cold, masklike features suddenly melt. During dinner he made a real effort to talk courteously to her. In half an hour she learned more about him than Sir Stephen had ever told her: she learned that he was Flemish, that he had business interests in the Belgian Congo, that he flew to Africa three or four times a year, that the mines brought in a great deal of money.

'What mines?' O said.

But he did not reply. He drank a lot, and his eyes were constantly fixed either on O's lips or on her breasts, whose movement could be discerned beneath the lace and whose painted nipples were sometimes visible through the wide-stitched mesh.

In the office, where O had taken him so that he could get a room, he said:

'Kindly have some whiskey sent up, as well as some bread and hors d'oeuvres.'

After he had possessed her in the same manner the Syrian had possessed Noelle, the same way in fact that O had been taken in the presence of Sir Stephen, after he had made her caress him, and as he was raising his riding crop for the third time, he seized O's hands, for she, in spite of herself, was trying to stop the descent of his arm. O read in his eyes a joy so violent that she knew then and there that she could expect no pity whatsoever from him (she had never expected any) but that also, and far more important, he would indeed come back.

XIII

It was rare for members of the Club or guests to come to the restaurant or bar accompanied by a woman, but it did happen. In fact, providing they were accompanied, women were not only allowed into the restaurant and bar at Roissy, but were also permitted to go up to the rooms. The man who brought them was not asked to pay any supplement, aside from their drinks and their meals, and was not asked to give their names. The only difference, under these circumstances, between Roissy and an ordinary short-time hotel was that, at Roissy, you were obliged to take, at the same time as you took a room, a girl. In the large, overheated room, along one of whose walls was a series of ferns and giant philodendrons which made the room smell faintly like a greenhouse, the women took off their overcoats, and sometimes the jackets of their suits. Their self-assurance, which perhaps concealed their uneasiness; their curiosity that they tried to disguise by their insolence; their smiles, which they tried to make haughty and contemptuous and which, in many cases, surely corresponded to real contempt, infuriated the girls and greatly amused the Roissy regulars, members or customers.

XIV

During the eight-day period that O was on duty in the restaurant, there were three women who came, on three different days. The third woman that O saw was a tall blonde who came in the company of a young man O had seen before at the bar. They sat down at one of the tables for which she was responsible, in a nook near the window. Almost immediately, one of the members of the Club named Michel joined them and made a sign for O to come over. Michel had slept with O once. When the man introduced him to the woman with him, O heard him add: 'My wife.' She wore a wedding ring studded with little diamonds and a dark, almost black sapphire. Michel bowed, sat down, and, after the *maitre d'* had taken their order, said to O, who was hovering close by:

'Bring the album for Madame.'

The young woman turned the pages of the album with a detached air, and would doubtless have flipped past the picture of O, pretending not to recognize her, when her husband said:

'Why, there's the girl waiting on us. It looks just like her.'

The woman raised her eyes to O and, without the trace of a smile, said:

'Oh, do you really think so?'

'Turn the page,' Michel said.

'Did you read what was on the back?' her husband said.

The woman closed the album without replying. But when O, who had gone to fetch their first course, came back to the table, she saw her talking heatedly, and Michel laughing. Then they fell silent each time she approached, but not always quickly enough, since as she was bringing coffee she heard the husband saying emphatically:

'Come on, now, make up your mind!'

Michel added something that O was unable to catch, whereupon the woman shrugged her shoulders.

In the room, the woman did not undress; with her dry hands she gently stroked O, who had the feeling of being touched by the claws of some large bird, then she watched while O caressed her husband before giving herself to him. When they departed, leaving her naked, they had neither beaten her, nor mistreated her, nor insulted her. They had always talked to her courteously. And yet she had never felt more humiliated in her life.

'Those bitches!' was Noelle's comment when O, whom Noelle had seen leave with the couple, finally responded to her persistent questions about what had happened, and the impression she had had of the whole affair, 'those bitches are as much prostitutes as we are, you'd better believe it, otherwise they wouldn't come here, but don't they think they're really something! If I had my way about it, I'd give them a slap or two they wouldn't soon forget!'

This feeling about the women who came to Roissy as visitors was as constant as it was unanimous. Whereas Noelle, and, moreover, all the other girls, and O, if they did upon occasion feel pangs of envy with respect to the girls brought to Roissy by their lovers, it was solely because of the attention their lovers paid them and not out of any feelings of real jealousy or bitterness. During her first stay at Roissy the year before, O had not had the slightest suspicion what desires she had awakened around her—desires to speak to her, to help her, to find out who she was, to kiss her—among the girls who, upon her arrival, had undressed her, washed her, arranged her hair, made her up, put on her corset and dress, who every day thereafter had taken care of her and had so vainly tried to strike up a conversation with her when they thought no one was looking, but always in vain; all the more vainly because she had never made any attempt to answer them.

When it was O's turn to perform what was referred to as 'room service,' that is to visit, together with Noelle, the bedrooms in the main enclosure, to help the girls who were lodged there to wash and dress, O was so upset by this kind of multiple transfer, by this several-copy incarnation of what she herself had been and what these visits kept bringing back to her, that she always crossed the threshold of the red rooms in a state of fear and trembling. For they were all red. What upset her the most was that she was never able to pinpoint with any degree of certainty which of the rooms had been hers. The third? The tall poplar tree rustled in front of the window. The pale asters, which would last till the end of autumn, were barely in flower. Was it the twenty-second or twenty-third of September? At any rate, the autumnal equinox. But the fifth room also had a poplar tree and its accompanying asters. It was occupied by a slender but well-proportioned girl, all white against the scarlet hangings, shaking, bearing on her thighs for the first time the purple furrows of the crop. Her name was Claude. Her lover was a thin young man who was holding her, by the shoulders, back on the bed, the way René had held her, and watching with obvious pleasure and passion as she opened her sweet burning belly to a man O had never seen, beneath whose weight the girl was moaning. Noelle washed her. O made her up, laced up her corset, and helped her on with her dress. She had sweet budding breasts with pink nipples, and well-rounded knees. She was silent, and lost. She, and the girls like her who belonged to members of the Club, girls who were shared exclusively by the members themselves, who gave themselves up to these unknown men in silence and who, as soon as they were deemed ready and sufficiently well-trained, would leave Roissy wearing the iron ring on their finger, there in the outer world to be prostituted by their lover, for his pleasure and his pleasure alone, these girls were, to the other girls at Roissy who were prostituted within the confines of the enclosure or without, for money, for the pleasure and benefit of the members of the Club and not solely for one man who loved them, objects of curiosity and endless conjecture. Would they ever come back to Roissy? Would they, if indeed they did come back, be locked behind the gate of the main enclosure or, if it were only for a few days, released from the rule of silence and put into the community? There was one girl whose lover left her in the main enclosure for six months, then took her away never to return. But O found Jeanne, who had remained for a year in the community, then had left, then had returned, that same Jeanne whom René had caressed in her presence and who had looked upon O with such envy and admiration. Beaten and chained like the other girls, the girls in the community were nonetheless free. Not free not to be beaten while they were there, but free to leave any time they so desired. But it was a fact that the very girls they treated most cruelly were the ones least likely to leave. Noelle stayed at Roissy for two months, then left and was gone for three months, returning after she had run out of money. But Yvonne and Julienne, who like O were flogged every day and, like O, as Noelle had predicted, often several times a day, Yvonne, Julienne, and O were as much prisoners of their own free will as were the girls of the main enclosure.

XV

After six weeks had passed, during which time O had clung faithfully to the hope, in spite of the deception of each new day, that Sir Stephen would come, O noted that if the members who were actually living at Roissy or who came back several days in a row were fairly common, the same generally held true for the customers. So it was that clear-cut preferences became established, or habits (as they did with the valets, to such a degree that often, in the refectory, the same valet would possess the same girl; thus, with O, whom José would order to sit astride him, with his hands holding her waist and buttocks, a pose in which O resembled, the way her back was slightly arched, the swooning woman held by the god Siva in Hindu statues), and O noted Carl's frequent return less because he sometimes came back four days in a row than because, each time, she tried to pry some information about Sir Stephen from him. He rarely talked of him, and whenever he did it was rather to explain to her what he, Carl, had said to Sir Stephen (about O) than what Sir Stephen had answered. He never left O any money, not once. Not that he was unaware of the practice. One night he had taken another girl upstairs with O, and the girl happened to be Jeanne. He had sent her back downstairs very quickly, keeping O with him, but he had sent Jeanne away with her hands stuffed with banknotes. For O, nothing.

Therefore she was completely in the dark when, one evening in October, instead of leaving as was his custom he told her to get dressed, waited until she was ready, and then handed her an oblong box of blue leather. O opened it. It contained a ring, a collar, and two diamond bracelets.

'You'll wear them in place of those you're now wearing,' he said to her, 'when I take you away.'

'Take me away?' said O. 'Where? You can't take me away.'

'I'm taking you to Africa first,' he said, 'then to America.'

'But you can't!' O repeated.

Carl made a movement with his hand that very clearly meant for her to keep quiet.

'I'm going to work it out with Sir Stephen,' he said. 'And then I'll take you with me.'

'But I don't want you to,' O cried, suddenly overwhelmed with a feeling of panic. 'I don't want you to. I don't. I don't!'

'Yes you do,' Carl said.

And O thought: I'll run away. Oh, not with him, oh, no; I'll run away.

The jewel case was open on the unmade bed, and the jewels, that O could not wear, sparkled among the disarray of the sheets, a fortune.

I'll run away, and I'll take the diamonds with me, O thought to herself, and she smiled at him.

XVI

He did not come back. Ten days later, while she was waiting, early one afternoon, in her gray and yellow dress of the first day, for a valet to come and open the little gate so that she could go into the library, she heard the sound of hurried steps behind her and turned around. It was Anne-Marie, who was holding a newspaper in one hand, which she handed to O. Anne-Marie was paler than O ever remembered seeing her.

'Look,' she said to O.

O's heart began to pound in her chest. On the first page a face, its expression blank, its mouth slightly parted, its eyes staring straight ahead: his face.

The headline read:

WHO IS THE NAKED WOMAN OF THE CRIME AT FRANCHARD?

The article went on to say:

'A group of Alpine mountain climbers who were practicing in the Franchard gorges in the forest of Fontainebleau, alerted by the barking of a dog, discovered the body of a man in the thickets. He had been killed by a bullet in the back of the neck. The unknown man, who appears to be a foreigner, had been stripped of all his papers. The only thing found on him was a woman's photograph which had been slipped or had fallen into the lining of his suitcoat. The woman was completely naked, and, according to certain signs, in all probability a prostitute. The police are looking for the woman.'

The description that followed left no doubt in O's mind that it was indeed Carl.

'Do you have any clear idea who might have done it?' said Anne-Marie.

'Oh, yes,' O said. 'Sir Stephen ... But you mustn't breathe a word.'

'You're wrong,' said Anne-Marie. 'But you don't have to say that Sir Stephen sent him to you. Still, you have to realize they may find that out anyway.'

When the police arrived at Roissy, Carl had already been identified not only by some laundry marks on his clothing but also by his tailor and the bellboys of his hotel. O was interrogated only as a material witness, and the questioning focused on the person of Sir Stephen. They knew that he was involved in some business dealings with Carl. What were these dealings? O did not know. After three hours of interrogation, O had still not provided them with any useful information, except to assert that she had not seen Sir Stephen for the past two months.

'Then for God's sake ask him,' she cried out at last in exasperation, 'and anyway, what difference does it make?'

'Don't you understand,' said one of them, 'that it was your fine-feathered friend who probably did away with the Belgian, and that's why he vanished. But between the theory and the proof ...'

They never did prove it. The theory was that Carl, who was known to have an interest in certain mines in Central Africa which produced some unspecified rare metals, had been getting ready to leave Europe after having negotiated—

without having any right to do so and after having been paid healthy sums of money (traces of which were later discovered in various bank accounts, but never the money itself)—with a number of foreign agents either for the concessions to the mines or for the products extracted from them. It was at this point that these agents, realizing they had been taken and that they had no recourse whatsoever in law, had taken their revenge. As for laying their hands on Sir Stephen ... As for knowing whether or not he would ever come back ...

'You're free now, O,' said Anne-Marie. 'We can remove your irons, your collar, and bracelets, and even erase the brand. You have the diamonds, you can go home.'

O did not cry, nor did she display any sign of bitterness. Nor did she answer Anne-Marie.

'But if you prefer,' Anne-Marie went on, 'you can stay on here.'

THE END

SOUTHERN DISCOMFORT
by RITA MAE BROWN

Hortensia Banastre is a Southern belle with a difference. At twenty-seven, she is trapped in a loveless marriage, unable to feel any emotion towards her indifferent, money-making husband or her two sons.

Then she meets Hercules, a fifteen-year-old black youth who dreams of becoming a prize-fighter. They fall in love and, throwing aside all social conventions, the two have a passionate affair – one that affects the lives of many people for years to come.

Peopled with some of the funniest, kindest and meanest characters around, SOUTHERN DISCOMFORT is an absorbing and marvellously funny novel, full of wit, wealth and whores.

'Raunchy, spirited and unrelentingly human'

Publishers Weekly

From the author of the bestselling RUBYFRUIT JUNGLE and SIX OF ONE.

0 552 12219 X   £1.95

DOCTOR LOVE
by GAEL GREENE

'The male fantasy of the 1980's'
New York Times Book Review

'DOCTOR LOVE would be a considerable book for any man to have written. Coming from a woman it is a tour de force'
Nancy Friday

Barney Kincaid, M.D., loves women. He loves loving women. Brilliant doctor, irascible watchdog of his hospital, loving father, devoted son, here is Barney Kincaid at forty-two. Caught up in the drama of high-risk medicine, he is a great lover who had never been in love.

Ecstatically he divides his time between Debra Teiger, his irrepressible playmate-in-kinkiness, and Lindsay, the wholesome WASP woman of his dreams.

Then, suddenly, he is forced to confront his own mortality. What seems like a heart attack isn't. The diagnosis is re-assuring but the shock of recognition sends Barney off on a voyage into his erotic past, a frenetic odyssey that almost destroys his career.

0 552 12201 7   £1.75

THE HOTEL NEW HAMPSHIRE
by JOHN IRVING

The Number One Bestseller by the author of THE WORLD ACCORDING TO GARP.

John Irving's novel – a hilarious family history with its own mythology and wisdom, takes its place alongside the great postwar American fictions: PORTNOY's COMPLAINT, CATCH-22, SLAUGHTERHOUSE FIVE and Irving's own THE WORLD ACCORDING TO GARP.

'A hectic gaudy saga with the verve of a Marx Brothers movie'
New York Times Book Review

'As good as, if not better than, GARP'
The Literary Review

NOW A MAJOR FILM.

0 552 12040 5   £2.50

TALES OF THE CITY
by ARMISTEAD MAUPIN

'Magically readable! This saga should continue for at least 1001 more nights'

Christopher Isherwood

YOU'LL LEAVE MORE THAN YOUR *HEART* IN THIS SAN FRANCISCO!

'I've never seen a street like that in my life, Mikey!'

He squeezed her arm, taking sudden pleasure in her innocence. 'It's an amazing city, Mama.'

Almost on cue, the nuns appeared.

'Herb, look!'

'Goddammit, Alice! Don't point!'

'Herb . . . they're on roller skates!'

Before their son could answer, the six white-coifed figures had rounded the corner as a unit, rocketing in the direction of the revelry on Polk Street.

One of them bellowed at Micahel.

'Hey, Tolliver!'

Michael waved half-heartedly.

The nun gave a high sign, blew a kiss, then shouted: '*Loved* your jockey shorts!'

'It's all as frothy as California surf, quick as a jazz joint pickup and bitchy as the morning-after brushoff'

Library Journal

'An epic uban Odyssey . . . poignantly funny . . . Rabelais in Tom Wolfe's clothing'

The Adovocate

0 552 11554 1   £2.95

CATCH-22
by JOSEPH HELLER

CATCH-22 has become a byword in its own time. It is a novel of enormous richness and art. It is deeply serious, yet at the same time, brilliantly funny. It is mentally gymnastic. It is without question one of the great novels of the century.

'Remarkable, mind-spinning, rave of a novel. Uniquely funny.'
Dail Mail

'Comic, macabre, knockabout, nightmarish, ironic, bawdy, illogical, formless, Shavian'

Books and Bookmen

'Blessedly, monstrously, bloatedly, cynically funny, and fantastically unique. No one has ever written a book like this'
Financial Times

'Wildly original, brutally gruesome, a dazzling performance that will outrage as many readers as it delights. Vulgarly, bitterly, savagely funny, it will not be forgotten by those who can take it'

New York Times

0 552 09755 1   £2.50

STREETS OF GOLD
by EVAN HUNTER

Born in the lusty world of Harlem's Italian quarter, Ike grew up to discover girls, his grandfather's love, and above all the exhilaration of music. His talent was prodigious – and he was blind . . .

Evan Hunter's brilliant novel tells it the way it is when you have ethnic roots so rich that all your life is coloured by them – and when you're driven by a talent that takes you all the way from success to disillusionment . . .

0 552 11963 6   £1.95

STORY OF O
by PAULINE RÉAGE

One of the most famous erotic novels of all time.

'A rare thing, a pornographic book well written and without a trace of obscenity'

Graham Greene

'A highly literary and imaginative work, the brilliance of whose style leaves no one in doubt whatever of the author's genius . . . a profoundly disturbing book, as well as a black tour-de-force'

Spectator

'Here all kinds of terrors await us, but like a baby taking its mother's milk all pains are assuaged. Touched by the magic of love, everything is transformed. STORY OF O is a deeply moral homily'

J. G. Ballard

'Cool, cruel, formalistic fantasy about a woman subjected – at the price of the great love of her life – to the gamut of male sado-masochistic urges'

Birmingham Post

0 552 08930 3   £1.95

EVEN COWGIRLS GET THE BLUES
by TOM ROBBINS

The novel of the year with the cast of the century!

Starring Sissy Hankshaw — flawlessly beautiful, almost. A small-town girl with big-time dreams and thumbs to match — hitchhiking her way into your heart, your hopes and your sleeping bag . . .

Featuring: Bonanza Jellybean and the smooth-riding cowgirls of Rubber Rose Ranch; Chink, lascivious guru of yams and yang; the Countess, homosexual tycoon of feminine hygiene; Julian, Mohawk by birth, asthmatic aesthete and husband by disposition; Dr Robbins, preventive psychiatrist and reality instructor . . .

Follow Sissy's amazing hitchhiking odyssey as she sets forth on a series of intellectual and erotic adventures that will bring tears to your eyes.

0 552 10513 9   £1.95

A SELECTED LIST OF TITLES
AVAILABLE FROM CORGI BOOKS

WHILE EVERY EFFORT IS MADE TO KEEP PRICES LOW, IT IS SOME-
TIMES NECESSARY TO INCREASE PRICES AT SHORT NOTICE. CORGI
BOOKS RESERVE THE RIGHT TO SHOW NEW RETAIL PRICES ON
COVERS WHICH MAY DIFFER FROM THOSE PREVIOUSLY ADVERTISED
IN THE TEXT OR ELSEWHERE.

THE PRICES SHOWN BELOW WERE CORRECT AT THE TIME OF GOING
TO PRESS (JANAUARY '85).

All these books are available at your book shop or newsagent, or can be ordered direct from the publisher. Just tick the titles you want and fill in the form below.

CORGI BOOKS, Cash Sales Department, P.O. Box 11, Falmouth, Cornwall.

Please send cheque or postal order, no currency.

Please allow cost of book(s) plus the following for postage and packing:

U.K. Customers—Allow 55p for the first book, 22p for the second book and 14p for each additional book ordered, to a maximum charge of £1.75.

B.F.P.O. and Eire—Allow 55p for the first book, 22p for the second book plus 14p per copy for the next seven books, thereafter 8p per book.

Overseas Customers—Allow £1.00 for the first book and 25p per copy for each additional book.

NAME (Block Letters) ....

ADDRESS ....

....